Love Means...

This story is written with heart. It is both bittersweet and uplifting, and reminds us that love can be generous and selfless and that a true family and sense of belonging don't necessarily require blood ties.

—Rainbow Reviews

This is one book that will make it to several keeper shelves to be read again and again.

—Literary Nymphs

Love Means... Courage

A story filled with laughter, sadness, joy, love and family...with all of the nuttiness that it entails. It will have you laughing, smiling, and reaching for the tissues in places. A definite keeper!

—Night Owl Reviews

A touching story that is full of heart and centered on what truly matters in partnerships and families regardless of the manner in which they come together ~ unconditional love, respect, understanding, support and above all courage.

—Rainbow Reviews

Love Means... No Boundaries

Andrew Grey

Dreamspinner Press

Published by
Dreamspinner Press
4760 Preston Road
Suite 244-149
Frisco, TX 75034
http://www.dreamspinnerpress.com/

Love Means... No Boundaries

Cover Design by Mara McKennen

ISBN: 978-1-61581-389-6

Printed in the United States of America
First Edition
February, 2010

eBook edition available
eBook ISBN: 978-1-61581-390-2

To Jackie, who inspired the entire idea in the first place.

PROLOGUE

COOL and crisp, the air braced his skin as he took one last ride through the quiet roads, the purple and white speed demon between his legs begging to be let loose, allowed to zoom with all haste. Putting his head down, he let it fly, let himself feel the freedom of the wind and road. No one was there. He was alone and loving it. Tomorrow he'd do what his mother wanted and put the bike away, but today he'd soar on its wings of metal, rubber, and pumping pistons.

The sun felt glorious, bright, and full, warming his leather as the wind cooled it. Everything was perfect—he could ride like this forever.

The car appeared suddenly in front of him, and he slowed, humphing at the slowpoke. But it wasn't moving. They weren't moving. He heard the crunch of metal, the bang, a pop. Swerving, he tried to avoid them. Too late. For a second he thought he could fly and then pain, warm wetness, blindness—nothing.

CHAPTER 1

"HOW was your class?" Joey strode into the kitchen, the back door banging behind him as he stomped his boots on the mudroom rug.

Eli turned from the sink where he was cleaning vegetables. "Good. The students are really great. I like the adult classes best. They're here to learn and work hard." He turned back around and went back to work. "Tomorrow I have the young kids. They're always a lot of fun too. It's the teenagers that are a pain... sometimes."

"Thanks for the warning. I'll be sure to make myself scarce." There was no way he was going to be around the young kids while they were getting their lesson.

Eli put down his vegetables and turned from the sink to look at Joey, huffing softly. "There's no need for that. Those kids love you and always ask about Mr. Joey."

His hand went to his face, fingers tracing the pink lines that he wished weren't there. "I just can't face the looks and the questions."

Joey saw Eli's eyes go sad. He knew that look, one he hated in everyone but Eli or Geoff. He knew that look from them was concern and not pity. He'd had all the pity he could stand. He'd avoided going to town because he just couldn't take the sad looks on everyone's faces and the tsks in their voices.

"You know they just want to help and that they feel for you."

"Pity." Joey spat the word and then felt bad about it. Eli was one of the best people he knew—always caring, never mean, or malicious in any way.

"Maybe a little, but they also care." Eli turned back to the sink. "You have a lot of people who care about you and don't give a"— Eli stopped for a second, and Joey saw his jaw go rigid—"rat's ass about the scars on your face because we don't see them anymore."

Joey stared at Eli's back as he worked. He knew how both Eli and Geoff felt. He just wished he could make himself believe it. But they hadn't been in the drugstore last month when a mother had pulled her children out of the store when she saw him walk in. "I know. It's just hard." The doctor had said that the scars would fade over time, and a plastic surgeon had worked on his face, so there was hope. But in the meantime, he just felt ugly.

Eli didn't look up as he continued making dinner. "How were the south fields? Did the rain wash away the seed?"

He sank into one of the kitchen chairs, grateful that Eli had let the subject drop. "Nope," Joey let himself smile as he slipped off his shoes. He still wasn't used to living in the farmhouse with Eli and Geoff, and he still felt he needed to be very careful of everything he did. "The seed's fine and in a few places it's beginning to sprout, so it looks like we're good."

"Geoff will be relieved." Joey could almost hear Eli smile as he worked. "I'm surprised he didn't go with you to check himself."

So was Joey, but it meant a lot to him that Geoff had trusted him to check on things, knowing he'd work to repair any damage the torrential downpour had caused. He'd been working on the farm since he was sixteen. After he returned from college, Geoff had offered him a job as crop manager after Frank Winters had retired. "I guess it was lucky that Pete and Hank needed help with the fences in the north pasture." As soon as the words passed his lips, he knew there was no luck involved. Eli had probably sent him out there to make sure Joey could do his job. He shook his head at Eli's back. The man knew his partner so well.

"How's your mom doing in Florida?"

"Getting settled. She already wants me to come down for a visit." Joey's mother had raised him single-handedly, and after he graduated from college, she sold the house and got a new job in Florida. She had said she was tired of the winters, and Joey was happy for her. She'd done her best and deserved some time to enjoy herself.

"You should. It might do you some good." Eli turned on the water and began rinsing the vegetables.

"I don't think so. Florida in June doesn't sound particularly appealing. Besides, there's plenty to help with around here." Joey took his job very seriously. He appreciated the responsibility that Geoff and Eli had given him, the faith they had in him, and there was no way he'd let them down. Ever. "Maybe I'll go down for a visit after the fall harvest. By then I'll be ready for some warmth and sun."

"Why don't you go get cleaned up? Dinner will be another hour, and you've been working since sunup." Joey didn't remind Eli that he'd been going since sunup as well.

Joey got up from the chair and walked to the sink. "Is there something I can do to help?"

"Go on. I've got this. Besides, you cook tomorrow night." Part of the arrangement when Eli and Geoff had offered him their guest room after his mother sold the house was that he would help with the cooking and cleaning. He'd readily agreed, and with Eli's help was starting to become a decent cook.

Joey left the kitchen and walked through the house. Sitting in one of the living room chairs and turning on the television, he began to relax—until the phone rang. Eli's voice drifted in from the kitchen, "Could you please get that?"

"Sure." Joey got up and reached for the phone.

"Geoff?"

He recognized the voice. "It's Joey, Mari." It was Geoff's sister, in Joey's opinion a wonderful lady. If he were straight, he'd have made a play for her, at least before….

"Hey, Joey, how's my brother treating you? Not working you too hard, is he?" Joey laughed in response. "Listen, is he around?"

"No, he's still out with the guys riding fence. Eli's in the kitchen making dinner." A crash sounded from the kitchen followed by a few expletives. Well, expletives in the sense that they were about as harsh as a man raised Amish would ever utter. "He seems to be having trouble with dinner."

"I need their help, and I'm a little desperate." He could hear the slight panic in her voice.

"What is it? I'll give them the message."

"The National Youth Symphony is arriving today, and one of my host families backed out. I need someone to take in one of the musicians, and I was hoping that Geoff and Eli would be willing to take him in." Mari had been talking about bringing this group to town the last time she was at the house. It seemed that Mari had called in a number of favors and pulled every string she could think of to get them to include the Ludington area in their tour. Joey knew she couldn't have something like this ruin it. "I've already got two girls staying with me, or I'd take him in."

5

"Hold on a minute. I'll ask Eli and be right back." Joey put down the phone and relayed the message to Eli who was wiping up the floor.

Eli barely looked up from his cleaning. "Tell Mari of course he can stay here. I'll make up a bedroom for him. Ask her when we need to pick him up." Joey hurried back to the phone.

Mari was thrilled and relieved. "Their bus arrives at the high school in fifteen minutes. I'll call the symphony coordinator and make sure that someone will be able to wait until you get there. Tell Eli thank you." She disconnected, and Joey relayed the message.

"Would you please pick him up for us? I need to finish this, and Geoff isn't back yet." Eli got up from the floor. "I know how you feel, and I wouldn't ask, but…."

Joey felt his insides start to churn, but he pushed it away as best he could. He owed Eli and Geoff a lot. He wasn't going to let his own insecurities get in the way. "No problem." Joey put his boots back on and headed outside. Getting into his car, he pulled out of the drive and headed to town. He hated doing this, but he hated the way he felt about it even more. *Grow a pair.* He tried to psych himself up, but all Joey could see was the reaction of some kid when he saw his face: some snooty teenager from some rich, well-to-do family who was given everything in life was going to take one look at him and then look away in disgust. "You may as well get used to it because it isn't going to change any time soon," he told himself as he drove down country roads lined with their freshly planted fields.

Approaching the outskirts of town, he slowed down and made his way to the high school, pulling into the long circular drive. He'd expected there to be a hoarde of people, but all he could see was a single bus and a woman standing next to a young man, holding what appeared to be a violin case. Pulling up behind the bus, he stopped the car and got out. The woman stepped forward, and to Joey's surprise, he saw none of the usual pity on her face. He almost wondered why. "Are you here for Robert Edward?" The woman looked relieved as she glanced across the parking lot to the only other car there. Two young women were talking together by the car. She'd obviously been waiting for him before taking them home.

"Yeah, I guess so. Mari didn't tell me his name. She just said that I needed to be here to pick up a young man." Joey wiped his hands on his pants as he turned to the man standing next to her. "I'm sorry I'm late. I'm Joey Sutherland."

"Robert Edward Jameson, but everyone calls me Robbie." He held out his hand, and Joey shook it, looking into Robbie's huge, blue eyes. He also noticed that Robbie smiled at him without a hint of pity or even curiosity. Joey actually felt some of his nervousness slip away.

"We should probably get your luggage loaded in the car." Joey popped the trunk and picked up a large suitcase, placing it in the trunk. He noticed that Robbie hadn't moved and hadn't offered to help. Shaking his head, he picked up the second case and loaded it, muttering under his breath, "What does he think I am, some sort of servant?" He slammed shut the trunk lid and walked back to where Robbie appeared to be waiting for him.

"If you two are all set, I'll be leaving. We'll see you at orchestra rehearsal tomorrow, nine sharp." The lady touched Robbie's shoulder as she began walking toward her car.

Robbie called after her, "Thank you, Mrs. Peters, for all your help." Joey noticed Robbie's Southern accent, and he smiled. The man was cute, and he sounded adorable. Too bad he was too full of himself to load his own luggage. He'd probably expect Joey to carry the bags upstairs and unpack them for him when he they got back.

"It's no problem, dear, you have a good time." Her voice trailed off as she got closer to her car.

"We should get going. Eli will have dinner ready soon." Joey walked around to the driver's side of the car and opened the door, expecting Robbie to do the same. When he didn't move, Joey walked back around to the passenger side and opened the door, "I'm not a chauffeur either."

"I didn't think you were a servant or a chauffeur, but I could use just a little help, if you don't mind." Robbie handed him his violin. "Would you please put that on the back seat?" Joey did as Robbie asked, wondering why he couldn't do it himself. Joey then waited and watched as Robbie reached into the pocket of the jacket hanging on his arm and pulled out something that looked like white folded sticks. With a slight flick of his wrist, the sticks rearranged themselves into a long, white cane. Joey blinked twice. *Shit and fuck.* Robbie was blind.

Joey felt completely insensitive and stupid, but he'd had no way of knowing. Those eyes seemed so big and bright. "Here, let me guide you to the car door." Joey gently touched Robbie's arm. "Step down from the curb and the car is straight ahead of you." Robbie tapped his cane on the ground as his other hand touched the car door, following it to the body of the car and then to the seat. "That's it. The seat is directly in front of you." Once he knew where he was, he easily sat down and pulled the car door closed, refolding the cane and setting it on his lap.

Joey got in as well and started the car, pulling around the drive and back out onto the road. He didn't know what to say—he felt like such a fool. How was he to know that Robbie was blind? But what he'd said had been rude, regardless of whether Robbie was blind or not. At least now he knew why Robbie didn't react to the scars on his face. "I'm sorry."

Robbie turned his head toward the sound of Joey's voice. "Why are you sorry?" Robbie smiled, and his face lit up. God, he was adorable, and it wasn't just his accent. The man was definitely cute. "You didn't know, and I'd be mad, too, if someone made me load the bags in the trunk without helping." That smiled widened. "Actually, I'm kind of grateful."

Joey didn't understand any of this. "For what?"

"You treating me like anyone else." Joey took a corner a little sharply, and Robbie leaned toward him. It took a few moments for him to correct his balance. Joey realized what had happened and slowed down. "Most people treat me different because I'm blind, but you treated me like anyone else."

"Well, you won't get special treatment around the farm, that's for sure." Even though Robbie couldn't see it, Joey smiled at him. "Everyone works pretty hard, and there won't be anyone who'll be able to stay with you all day long. You'll be on your own for some of the time."

"A farm?" Damn, Robbie's smile widened farther, if that was possible. "We're going to a farm, like a real farm with horses and cows and stuff?"

"Well, yeah. Laughton Farms is the biggest operation in the county. We have almost three thousand acres now, with fifteen hundred head of cattle, as well as horses." Joey went on about the farm, telling Robbie about the barns and the dogs. "Geoff and his partner Eli own and manage the farm together."

Robbie's face registered confusion for a second. "Partner as in business partners?"

"No," Joey corrected, "partners as in partners in life."

"Oh."

THAT little revelation surprised Robbie, but he didn't have time to dwell on it. Instead he filed it away to ponder later as the car bounced and swayed, and Robbie did his best to go with the movement instead of against it. Since he couldn't see anything, he didn't know what to prepare for, which was normal for him. Curves sent him swaying unexpectedly in either one direction or the other. As they turned, he felt the warmth of the sun on his face and fished around in his jacket pocket for a pair of sunglasses and put them on to protect his eyes.

"We should be getting to the farm in a few minutes."

"Good." Robbie turned and smiled at his companion. He'd never considered the possibility of staying on a farm. The thought was definitely exciting but a little daunting as well. He knew there'd be a lot of things that were new to him and that he'd have to be careful, but he also hoped there might be the chance to experience something new. "When we get there, will you be able to show me around?"

"Show you… shit." Robbie could hear the embarrassment in Joey's voice. "I'm sorry."

"Would you stop apologizing?"

"Yeah, okay." The car lurched slightly, and Robbie bounced on the seat, glad he was wearing a seatbelt. "Sorry." Robbie felt the car slow, and the bumpiness evened out.

"I'll need someone to show me around the house so I can learn where everything is."

"You'll learn where things are that fast?"

"Usually. It doesn't really take long. As long as you don't rearrange the furniture or move the bathroom to another part of the house, I should be fine." Robbie heard Joey chuckle, and he chuckled in return, glad Joey had gotten his humor. He'd stayed with a number of families on the tour, and some of them had been so uptight the entire time that he couldn't get comfortable. Yes, he was blind, but he wasn't helpless.

"How do you do it? Learn where things are so fast?"

He liked the sound of Joey's voice—mellow and smooth, and his accent was cute too. Robbie shrugged. "You do what you have to." Further explanation was cut off by the familiar Mozart ringtone. Reaching into his pocket, he pulled out his phone. "Hi, Mama."

"Did you make it okay?" Her voice conveyed her usual exaggerated concern.

"Yes. I'm just fine. We're on our way to the house now. We should be there soon."

"Make sure they show you around so you can pace off the rooms, and don't let them put you too far from the bathroom." Robbie shook his head and rolled his sightless eyes, wishing she could see. His mother really hated when he did that. It creeped her out for some reason, which of course was why he did it in the first place.

"I'll be fine, Mama. You don't need to worry." He was twenty-two, for God's sake, and she still treated him like a baby. "We're pulling into the drive now." He felt the car slow and heard the turn signal. Even if they were just making a turn, it was an excuse to get her off the phone.

"Okay, honey. I'll talk to you later." He hung up the phone and slipped it back in his pocket.

"Your mom?" Robbie heard the crunch of gravel under the wheels and figured they were turning into the drive.

"Yeah." The woman called at least three times a day just to check on him. After six weeks, it was getting to be a little much. He felt the car pull to a stop and heard the engine quit. "Is this it?"

"Yup. I'll get you out and into the house and come back for your things, if that's okay."

"I appreciate it." Robbie waited as he heard Joey's seatbelt click.

"No problem." He unfastened his own seatbelt, fumbling slightly with the buckle.

The driver's door creaked a little as it opened, and he felt the car rock slightly as Joey got out. The door closed again, the car vibrating from the impact. Footsteps on the gravel signaled Joey's approach, and then the door opened, and he felt Joey's hand on his arm. "Step out. The drive's gravel, so you'll want to make sure you're steady." Letting Joey guide him, Robbie stood and extended his cane.

"Would you bring my jacket?"

"Sure, hang on a second." He felt Joey's hand leave his arm, but a few seconds later it was back, warm and soft on his skin with a grip that wasn't tight, but firm and reassuring. "Take a few small steps so I can close the door." Robbie complied, and he heard the car door thunk closed. Joey guided him patiently around the car and up to the house, his voice keeping up a steady, reassuring narrative. "Let me open the door, and then there's three steps into the house."

"Just a second." Joey continued holding Robbie's arm as he inhaled deeply. The scent of horses, hay, straw, and manure all assaulted his senses at the same time. He'd never smelled anything like it. "What is that?"

"What?" He heard Joey sniffing the air and couldn't help smiling.

It was wonderfully overwhelming, and he was having trouble distinguishing between everything. "Are there horses nearby?" He could hear what he thought might be whickering, and he could feel the pounding of what might be hooves.

"There's a corral about fifty feet away."

Robbie was starting to get excited. "Was there a horse running?"

"Yeah. How'd you know?" He heard what he thought was amazement in Joey's voice.

"I could feel the ground vibrate from its hooves." Robbie turned and began sniffing all around him. "This is more amazing than I ever dreamed." He didn't want to move from this spot. The scents, the sounds, the vibrations he could feel through his feet, all combined in a sensory delight.

"We should go inside. Eli will have dinner ready. But I promise, after I show you around the house, I'll take you to the barn so you can meet some of the horses." There was that touch again, firm and reassuring.

Tapping the ground with his cane, Robbie felt where the step was and lifted his foot, slowly climbing the stairs into the house. Once inside he jumped slightly as the screen door banged closed, and then a whole new array of aromas and sounds assailed him. From the smells surrounding him, he assumed he was in the kitchen. He was going to enjoy his time on the farm.

"Is this Robert Edward?" A new voice asked, and he felt footsteps approach.

"This is Eli," Joey said, and Robbie extended his hand to feel a calloused one grip it.

"Please, call me Robbie."

"It's good to meet you." He sensed a slight hesitation in Eli's voice and assumed he hadn't known that their guest was going to be blind. The back door opened and banged closed. Then he heard heavy, booted footsteps on the floor. "Geoff, take off your boots." Robbie tried not to smile at the mild scolding as he heard the man sit down and the boots clunk on the floor.

"Geoff, this is Robbie."

"Pleased to meet you." The man's grip was firm. He could almost hear the smile in his voice, and Robbie knew without a doubt that the welcome was genuine. "I hope you'll like it here."

"I'm sure I will." Damn—he was so excited. He was grinning like a fool.

"Dinner will be ready in ten minutes." He immediately placed Eli's voice and felt Joey's hand on his arm again. New people were always blank to him. So many cues were visual, and he missed out on those, so it took him time to get an impression of people. That was one of the strange things about Joey: he'd gotten an impression of him right away, and it wasn't the one he'd have expected from his earlier grumbling. It was from his touch, which was strong, yet gentle. He knew just how Robbie liked to be touched. Robbie suppressed a shudder and stopped himself from going down that path. He was just being silly, and he shouldn't be thinking about Joey that way.

There was one thing he was sure of—he was going to have a good time at the farm. These people, this place, it seemed special somehow. He wasn't sure why he felt that, but he did. Robbie firmly believed in positive and negative energy. Not being able to see, he was particularly attuned to it. And this place, these people, radiated positive energy. Well, everyone except Joey. His energy wasn't negative, more like painful. He could hear it in his voice, too, just below the surface, and he wondered what could have caused it.

"I'll guide you to the bathroom so you can wash up, and after dinner I'll show you around and get your things up to your room." Joey brought him to the bathroom, and after washing up, Robbie was able to retrace his steps back to the table using his cane. Even though Joey said nothing, he could feel him close by, watching, but not hovering. Sitting at the table, a plate was placed in front of him, and he heard Joey's smooth voice softly explain where everything was located, and he felt his hand on his, guiding it to his glass. Every time Joey touched him, he felt something. He wasn't sure what it meant, but he definitely liked it.

Love Means ... NO Boundaries

"I'm not a particularly graceful eater," Robbie said softly, hoping only Joey could hear. "I tend to spill food off the plate and don't realize it."

He felt Joey's hand on his shoulder. "Don't worry about anything; just enjoy. Eli's a great cook." Robbie took him at his word and ate, enjoying every bite.

At first the conversation centered on him, with everyone asking a ton of questions, but then the conversation shifted to the business of the farm, and Robbie ate slowly and listened, taking in everything: how the cattle were doing, their plans for getting in enough hay, the condition of the fields and seed. It felt so normal, and Robbie found he was smiling to himself, thinking *they're treating me like anyone else.* In his experience, there weren't many people who did that, and he really appreciated it.

His phone ringing interrupted dinner, and he put down his fork and fished it out of his pocket. "Hi, Mama."

"Are you doing okay, honey?"

"I'm fine. Mama, we're having dinner." These calls were really getting on his nerves.

"You know you have a delicate digestion. I hope they're feeding you things you can eat."

"I'm just fine, Mama. I need to finish eating so they can show me around, and I have rehearsal all morning tomorrow, so I won't be able to answer the phone."

"Okay, good night, honey. Call me after rehearsal." She hung up, and Robbie went back to his dinner, the conversation picking up where it left off, to Robbie's relief and gratitude.

After dinner Joey guided him all around the house, highlighting the placement of all the furniture, the locations of the bathrooms, and everything he could need. "I'm going to get your bags, and then I'll take you up to your room." Robbie settled into one of the chairs and let the sounds of the house roll around him. Eli was in the kitchen doing dishes, and then Robbie heard a soft giggle and a splash. He figured Geoff had joined him and that the dishes would wait. A soft moan drifted to his ears, and he smiled as another splash was followed by definite sounds of kisses. The back door opened and banged shut, heavy footsteps walking through the kitchen. "I've got your suitcases, and I'll take them upstairs, but I thought you might want this." Robbie felt his violin case rest on his lap, and his hands wrapped around it instinctively. "I'll be right back." Robbie heard heavy clomps on the stairs followed by doors opening and closing and clomps again.

Robbie felt Joey approach, and then a hand touched on his arm. "I'll help you up the stairs." Just like before, he guided him up through the rooms and up the stairs. "Your room is at the top of the stairs to the right. My room is across the hall. There's a bathroom right next door." He felt Joey lead him there, explaining where all the important things were before leading him back to the bedroom. "Your suitcases are on the bed, and I put your jacket on the footboard." Slowly, he led Robbie around. "There's a nightstand on either side and a dresser to your right." Robbie ran his hand over the smooth wood, before feeling down the front and pulling out a drawer.

"Thank you."

"Do you need help putting your things away?"

"No, if I do it myself it's easier for me to find things later." He began opening one of the suitcases, "I could use your help with my tux though." Robbie lifted the garments out of the case and handed them to Joey."

"No sweat, I'll hang it up for you." He heard Joey move around the room and the closet door opened and closed. "Do you want to come back downstairs?"

Love Means ... NO Boundaries

Robbie shook his head. "No, I'll finish unpacking and then go to bed."

"Okay, I'll get you up for breakfast. Good night." Robbie heard Joey leave the room, closing the door behind him as he continued with his unpacking. Yes, indeed, he really was going to like it here. These were good people.

It took him a while to unpack and make sure he was familiar with everything in the room. He also made a couple trips to the bathroom to make sure the path was engrained before getting undressed and climbing into bed.

Robbie was tired, but his mind just wouldn't shut off, so he lay there listening and wondering about Joey. The man fascinated him, and he had no logical reason why. Footsteps on the stairs told him the others were going to bed as well, and after some movement in and out of the bathroom, the house quieted down, and still he just lay there, thinking.

Then he heard it. Whispers and soft moans drifted to his ears through the wall. He knew what it was and tried to block it out but couldn't. He felt like an intruder as he strained to hear. The sound of lovemaking suddenly made him feel very lonely. He'd never touched anyone that way, and he wondered very much what it felt like. There were a lot of things he'd never done, but sometimes he wondered if he'd ever have someone that was his, just his. Someone who'd touch him and love him the way Geoff and Eli loved each other. Finally, his own fatigue took over, and he drifted off to sleep.

CHAPTER 2

THE sun was barely up when Joey woke. His body wouldn't let him sleep any longer. When he'd first come to the farm full-time, it had been difficult for him to get up so early, but now, he couldn't sleep in. Throwing back the covers, he got up and went to the bathroom to clean up. He could hear Geoff and Eli already up, moving around downstairs. When he passed Robbie's door, he noticed it was open slightly, and soft snores were coming from the room.

"Rex, get out of there." He saw the dog lift his head from the foot of Robbie's bed before putting it back down and closing his eyes. "Fine." Joey smiled as he backed away from the door, letting both Robbie and the dog sleep. After a quick cleanup, he headed to the kitchen for some of Eli's coffee. "Morning." Joey yawned as he poured himself a cup.

"Morning. What's on your agenda for today?" Geoff sat at the table finishing his coffee before starting his chores.

"I need to check on all the fields, and someone needs to take Robbie to his rehearsal at nine." He saw the look that passed between Geoff and Eli, wondering what it was about but knowing better than to ask. Those two seemed to be able to communicate volumes with just a glance.

"I've got fences to check, and Eli has classes and lessons for most of the day. Would you be able to make sure Robbie gets where he needs to go?" Geoff sipped his coffee as Eli placed a plate in front of him and put one on the table for Joey.

Joey nodded his agreement. "When does Len get back?" Joey sat down and began eating.

"A few days. He and Chris should be done with their tour of the wine country by then." Geoff smiled and continued eating. Joey said nothing and continued eating. Len had been like a father to him. When Joey was sixteen, he'd asked how much riding lessons cost, and Len had arranged for him to work in exchange for those lessons. That was a momentous day. Len started off as his instructor and ended up as a close friend who acted like the father he'd never had, with both Geoff and Eli treating him like a brother.

Geoff finished off his breakfast and took his plate to the sink, giving Eli a soft kiss and a "thank you" before heading out to the barn. "You should wake Robbie up. It might take him some time to get ready," Eli commented as he looked up from his breakfast to watch Geoff leave.

"You're right." Joey finished up, and after thanking Eli, placed his dishes in the sink and made his way upstairs. "Robbie." Rex looked up from where he was sleeping, but made no move to get up, and neither did the sleeping form beneath the covers. "Robbie." Joey walked to the side of the bed and gently rocked one of his shoulders. "Robbie, you need to get up." Joey saw those big blue eyes open and watched as Robbie sat up in bed, the covers pooling around his waist.

"What time is it?" Robbie sounded groggy.

Joey wanted to answer, tried to answer. His lips moved, his mouth formed words, but he couldn't speak them. All he could do was look at Robbie's smooth chest. Rich honey skin, tawny nipples. He almost reached out to stroke, but he managed to stop himself, finally finding his voice. "It's a little after seven." Thank God Robbie couldn't see him standing there gawking at the man, and with a smile, he realized he could continue to look without repercussions. "We weren't sure how long you'd need to get ready, so I got you up early. I hope it's okay."

Robbie smiled, and Rex slunk up the bed, bumping his nose beneath Robbie's hand for scratches. "Have you been keeping me company?" Robbie scratched the big mutt before pushing back the covers, slowly getting to his feet, and feeling his way to the dresser.

"Do you need anything?"

"No. I should be fine."

"Call if you need anything." Joey left the room and went downstairs to the office. He'd developed detailed crop plans for all the fields, and he wanted to take them with him so he could record how each of the fields was germinating. Sitting at Geoff's desk, he reviewed his plans while listening in case Robbie needed anything.

He was just finishing up when he heard tentative footsteps on the stairs followed by the rush of doggie feet. "I'm in the office," Joey called out, and a few minutes later he saw Robbie's smiling face poke through the doorway.

"Is there time for breakfast?"

"Sure." He put his papers in a folder and took them with him to the kitchen where he made Robbie a quick breakfast. As Robbie finished eating, he pressed a button on what looked like a watch, and Joey heard a mechanical voice say, "Eight forty-five."

"That's cool."

Love Means ... NO Boundaries

"We should go. How long will it take us to get to the auditorium at the community college?" Robbie raised himself out of the chair and picked his cane up off the table.

"About two minutes. It's across the street." Joey put his hand on Robbie's elbow. "Let me get your violin, and I'll help you to the car.

A few minutes later, Robbie was in the car with his instrument resting on his lap, and Joey drove them across the street, pulling up in front of the auditorium. "Just a minute." He put the car in park and opened his door, walking around the car and opening Robbie's door. "I'll help you get inside."

As Robbie stepped out of the car, the door to the auditorium swung open and a tall, wiry young man rushed across the pavement. "Robbie." Reaching them he took Robbie's arm. "I'll help him in."

Before Joey could respond, the young man looked up at him, and he heard the intake of breath before the expression on his face changed to the surprised look Joey was used to seeing on people's faces when they saw him the first time. Then the expression was gone, but Joey felt a wave of disappointment shoot through him.

This had been the first morning in a long time that he hadn't woken to the same feeling of self-pity. He'd actually been able to forget about the scars, forget what he looked like now, until he saw the look on the man's face—and for a split second he absolutely hated him. Joey knew it wasn't his fault, and the feeling passed, but for a split second....

Robbie's voice pulled him out of his emotions. "Arie, this is Joey. Joey, this is a friend from back home, Arie."

The young man extended his hand. "Robert Edward Hawkins." Joey shook the offered hand and noticed that Arie's voice sounded normal, but the look on his face was one Joey couldn't place.

"Isn't Robbie's name Robert Edward as well?"

"Yeah, every family has a Robert Edward where we come from, named after Robert E. Lee. That's why I go by Arie." Again, something was off, but Joey couldn't quite place it. The voice sounded helpful, but something was off between the words and the expression.

"Oh," Joey didn't know what to say, and he certainly didn't know what to make of Arie "How long do you expect rehearsal to last?"

"We should be done at eleven," Arie said as he led Robbie toward the building. Joey watched as they walked away, Arie's arm on Robbie's, a weird look on his face that he couldn't place. Joey got back in the car and was about to pull away when he stopped the car again, looking back toward the now closed door. There was something that just wasn't quite right about this Arie. Taking his foot off the brake, he pulled away from the auditorium.

Joey's impulse was to drive back to the farm and go up to his room and hide, but he forced himself to work, turning his car down the road and toward the first of many fields he needed to inspect. When it was time to pick up Robbie, he found himself parked outside the auditorium. Instead of waiting, he went inside and heard rich, full music drifting through the halls. Quietly, he cracked open one of the doors and slipped inside, sitting in one of the chairs in the dark portion of the auditorium.

His gaze went directly to Robbie, sitting in one of the front chairs, his violin under his chin, bow gliding back and forth over the strings. He didn't know the piece they were playing, but he could immediately tell that Robbie enjoyed it. There was this rapturous look on the young musician's face, and he found himself staring at him, watching every nuance, every movement he made.

The music came to an end, and Robbie's expression relaxed, the violin lowered before resting on his lap. He knew the director was giving instructions, and he saw Arie, who was sitting next to Robbie, lean close and whisper something to him. Robbie didn't react, but Joey saw the expression on Arie's face clearly, and he recognized it. Arie was in love with Robbie. He watched as Arie touched Robbie gently on the hand, stroking his skin. The gesture was as plain to Joey as Arie standing up and yelling to everyone that he was in love with Robbie.

Joey felt his stomach clutch in disappointment for a split second and release again. Joey had no claim on Robbie. Hell, he'd just met the man yesterday, so why was he feeling so let down? He thought he might have been jealous, but no, what he was feeling was more like general unfairness. Since his accident, people shied away from him when they first met him, but Robbie hadn't, for obvious reasons.

A soft tapping reached his ears as the conductor tapped his baton. He watched as Robbie lifted his violin, and they began playing again. It didn't take long for that rapturous look to overtake Robbie's face again, and Joey found himself wondering what it would be like to put that look on Robbie's face in another way. His imagination took off, and he began to picture what Robbie might look like laid out on his bed, smooth skin against his sheets, the man vibrating with excitement, that same rapturous look on his face as he came.

Joey stifled a soft moan and brought himself back to the here and now as the orchestra finished up the piece. Then he heard the conductor giving instructions again before dismissing the musicians.

Joey waited in the back of the auditorium and watched as Robbie lovingly packed up his instrument. It looked like Arie tried to guide Robbie off the stage, but Robbie seemed to shake him away before extending his cane and gingerly but unerringly making his way toward the stairs. Arie continued to hover, but Robbie made his way alone off the stage and up the aisle. Joey smiled and shook his head. The man was independent; he had to give him that.

Joey stood up, "Robbie." He said the name softly, almost reverently, knowing he'd be heard.

"Did you hear us?" Robbie approached, following the sound of his voice.

"I sure did."

"What did you think?"

"Beautiful." As Joey said the word, he realized he was answering Robbie's question and expressing what he thought of Robbie all at once. Joey stood up and Robbie reached for his arm. As Joey led him out of the auditorium, he turned back toward the stage and shivered when he saw the look on Arie's face. Venomous didn't begin to describe it. As soon as Arie realized he was being watched, the look vanished. "I parked in the lot. I can get the car or we can walk."

Robbie looked up at him, a smile on his face. "Let's walk. I spend way too much time inside both cars and houses." Joey led them outside and down the walk to the parking lot. "I have some things I need to do this afternoon." He wasn't quite sure how to ask what he wanted to. "Do you want to rehearse or something?"

"Is there anything I can do to help?" He stopped walking and stood in the middle of the walk, slipping his sunglasses on and tilting his face to the sun.

Joey watched Robbie soak up the sun's warmth. "You know, there just might be. Have you ever planted a garden?"

Robbie's response was a deep laugh. "You have to be kidding. I've never gotten my hands dirty except when I've fallen down."

"I need to get the vegetable garden planted now that all the other fields are planted and growing." They began moving toward the car again.

"I'm game if you're game. I don't know how much I can help, but I'm willing if you are."

Love Means ... NO Boundaries

They reached the car, and Joey opened the door. "Then we need to get some lunch, because we have a very busy afternoon ahead of us." Robbie settled on the seat, and Joey closed the door and got into the driver's seat.

"Just what is it you have planned?"

"From the sound of it, lots of things you've never done before." Joey took Robbie's arm reassuringly. "I promise I won't let anything happen to you." He wasn't quite sure how Robbie was going to help him in the garden, but he'd figure something out. Blind or not, Joey figured Robbie could do just about anything he set his mind to, and if he was willing to try helping him in the garden, who was he to turn down help, sighted or not? Starting the car, he pulled out and headed toward the farm.

ROBBIE changed clothes and made his way down to the kitchen, pleased at how easily he was finding his way around the house. "Are you ready?" Joey's voice rumbled around him.

"Yeah." He felt Joey's hand in his arm.

"Then let's go. We have plenty of work to do." He let Joey lead him outside and across the yard. "I already brought the plants and seeds out, so we should be all ready."

"Okay, what is it you want me to do?" He could feel the ground under his feet begin to give, like it was soft.

"Sit down, and I'll explain." Robbie complied, sitting on the soft earth. "In front of you is a section of the garden that I've staked out. The stakes are in a grid pattern, that's three by three with two feet between each stake." Robbie felt Joey take his hand and place it on a stake. "That's the corner." Robbie felt Joey move his hands in the direction of the stakes. "And here's the middle. We'll plant this one first. All you need to do is dig a hole where each stake is and I'll hand you a tomato plant that you place in the hole and push the dirt around."

"That's it?" He felt the handle of what he assumed was the trowel being placed in his hand.

"Yes. You ready to try?"

Robbie smiled as he reached to the center stake and dug a shallow hole. "Is that good?" He felt a small plastic container being placed in his hand.

"That's perfect. Now put your fingers across the top of the pot with the plant sticking between them and turn it over. It should fall out. Then place the plant in the hole and put the soil around it."

Robbie did as Joey instructed and felt the small plant slip from the pot. Locating the hole he'd dug with his hand, he placed the plant in it and slid the soil around it. "Is that it?"

"That's wonderful." Robbie could hear the smile on his face. "Do you think you can do the others? All you need to do is stay on the outside of the stakes."

"Yeah, I think I can." The realization that he really did believe he could took him by surprise.

"I'll place a plant next to each stake; that way you won't need to find them."

Robbie moved outside the grid and located the corner stake, reconfirming with Joey before getting started. He'd just begun digging the hole when his phone went off. Robbie groaned softly and put down the trowel and dug the phone out of his pocket. "Hi, Mama." The woman seemed to be calling more and more often.

"Hi, honey, how was rehearsal?" Her voice sounded so normal.

"It went well. He's got us working on a new piece."

Love Means ... NO Boundaries

"Did you have time to learn it?" He could hear her getting concerned and knew she was feeling protective.

"I did okay. I've got a copy, and I'll learn it over the next few days." He knew what he needed to do and his hackles went up.

"He should be giving you the music earlier so you can learn it."

"Mama, it's fine. Was there something you wanted? I'm kind of busy."

"Doing what? Where are you?"

"I'm outside."

"Do you have your sunglasses on?"

Jesus, she was getting worse. "Of course. Is there something you wanted?" His voice became firm, trying to get her off the phone.

"Nothing other than to see how you were."

"I'm fine." She continued to prattle on about something, but Robbie was no longer listening. "Bye, Mama." He hung up the phone and put it back in his pocket. He could really care less about whatever benefit his mother was planning now. Feeling around, he located the trowel and went back to work. He finished the second plant and moved on to the next.

Joey finished setting the tomato plants by the stakes. "Can I ask you a question?"

Robbie moved and sat next to the stake and began to dig. "Sure."

"Were you born blind?"

"No. When I was twelve, I got really sick, and they thought I wasn't going to live. I did, but I lost my sight. The disease damaged the optic nerves." He continued working.

"So you know what it's like to see?"

"Yeah, I do, sort of." Robbie stopped what he was doing and knelt on the warm ground. "In some ways it would be easier if I'd have been born blind. Then I wouldn't know what I'm missing. But yeah, I know what it's like to see. I understand most sight-based references and what colors are." Robbie explained further. "Most blind people can't understand color because it's strictly based on sight."

"How do you learn music if you can't see it?"

"I get it in Braille. But I have to memorize it, because it takes two hands to play."

"Wow," Robbie heard the wonder in the other man's voice. "That's awesome. It must be wonderful to be so talented." Robbie went back to work, feeling the ground vibrate slightly as Joey moved around behind him.

"What is it you're planting?" He heard the sound of something shaking.

"Carrots." The shaking stopped. "I've already planted the cucumbers, and I'll plant squash, beans, some sweet corn, and radishes." Robbie felt that Joey had stopped working and was looking at him. "You're doing great."

"Thanks." He finished another plant, the soil feeling good in his hands, and moved to the next stake. "Can I ask you a question?"

"Turnabout is fair play." Robbie heard a note of apprehension in Joey's voice.

"Did something happen to you?" Robbie finished smoothing the soil around the tomato. "When Arie saw you today, he gasped, and I heard a slight gasp yesterday from Mrs. Peters."

He heard Joey take a deep breath and release it slowly. "I was in an accident and hurt my face. A couple of cars hit each other, and

Love Means ... NO Boundaries

I couldn't stop my bike in time. I was lucky. I ended up with a few broken bones, but my face got cut up pretty bad."

"I take it from the strain in your voice that you don't want to talk about it." It was obvious to Robbie that he didn't, but he couldn't help thinking that talking about it might be good for his new friend.

"Not really."

Robbie nodded his head and continued working. Moving to the last stake. "What do you want me to do next?"

"You want to plant corn?" He could hear the tension leave Joey's voice.

"Sure." He was having a great time. He rarely got to do things with other people. At home if he needed something, people often got it for him, and when he practiced, he was alone. This was different and a lot of fun. Finishing up the planting, he sat back and waited for Joey. He didn't have to wait long, and he felt that gentle, firm touch on his arm, helping him to his feet and guiding him to the next location in the garden. Joey's hand slid along the skin of his arm and Robbie felt something different, something he'd never felt before. He became excited, from a simple, soft caress. He felt Joey guiding him back to the ground, and he had to be careful because his pants were suddenly really tight. Every time Joey touched him, he reacted. He had to get his thoughts on something else.

Thankfully Joey didn't seem to notice, and he went about telling Robbie what he needed to do to plant the corn.

They spent the remainder of the afternoon working together in the garden, sharing stories and jokes. It had been a long time since Robbie had laughed with anyone like he did with Joey. It was great working together, and he just wished he'd be around to see the fruits of their labors, so to speak.

"You ready to go in for a while, maybe get something to drink?" Robbie nodded his agreement and Joey led him back inside and into the kitchen. Robbie couldn't remember feeling so tired and exhilarated—or spending the afternoon in the sunshine and fresh air.

"Did you have a good day?" Geoff asked, as he moved around the room. Robbie thought Eli was there, as well, but he wasn't sure.

"Yeah. I did." He smiled in the direction of the voice, hoping he saw it.

"I'm glad." He heard Geoff bring him a cool drink, placing his hand against the sweating glass. "I'll be back in about an hour." Robbie sipped the fresh lemonade and sighed as it slipped down his parched throat. He heard Eli respond, confirming for Robbie what he'd suspected.

A hand rested gently on his shoulder, and Robbie recognized Joey's touch. "I'm going to get cleaned up. Do you need anything?"

"No, I'm good." The hand slipped away, and Robbie felt a momentary loss as the warmth went with it. He heard retreating footsteps through the house. Robbie took a huge gulp of the tart lemonade, imagining the bite felt like a shot of liquor, trying to screw up his courage. "Mr. Eli, are we alone?"

"Yes we are. That must be difficult, trying to keep track of who's in the room." There was a caring kindness in his voice that Robbie found himself responding to.

"Can I ask you a question?" Robbie set the glass on the table, feeling carefully to make sure he didn't spill. He felt self-conscious enough and didn't want to add a drippy mess to the list.

A chair scraped across the floor, and he heard Eli sit down across the table from him. "Of course, what's on your mind?"

Robbie took a deep breath, steeling his nerves. "How did you know you were," he swallowed wondering how he could get the word out, "gay." He whispered the last word like it was the worst curse word in the history of curse words.

He felt Eli take his hand and squeeze gently. "It's perfectly fine to ask whatever you want to ask here." He waited, hoping Eli would continue. "I'm probably not the best person to ask because my experience is different. I was raised Amish, and being gay was unthinkable. But I wasn't happy and couldn't figure out why. My family suggested some time away from the community, and I intended to use it to figure things out." Robbie listened intently as the chair scraped on the floor again, and Robbie listened for other movement, but the house remained quiet except for the sound of water running upstairs. "I was lucky. The first night, I didn't have a place to stay and happened upon a barn. Geoff found me sleeping in a stall and gave me a job. Best day of my life."

"But how...." Robbie's frustration seemed to bubble out, and he felt Eli's reassuring hand on his.

"When I met Geoff, I felt happy, peaceful, and I just knew almost from the first. Deep down I knew it was right. The hard part was allowing myself to accept it." Robbie felt Eli's reassurance again. "Geoff helped me understand that being gay isn't about liking boy bits or girl bits—it's about who you fall in love with, who you want to spend the rest of your life with, and I couldn't imagine spending the rest of my life with anyone other than Geoff."

The deep emotion in Eli's voice caught Robbie off guard for a second. "Do your parents know about you?"

"No, and they never can for their own sake. They'd be guilty by association, and some in their community would shun them. There are already people in the community who treat them differently because I left. I love Geoff, and my life is here, but I don't want them hurt because of it. Do your parents know about you?"

"God no!" Robbie let his head bow forward. "I can't be gay, I just can't." He thought he was going to start to cry, and he held it in because that would be just too embarrassing.

"It's not something you get to choose, but it is something you can choose to accept." Robbie felt Eli's fingers lift his chin. It was such a strange gesture for him because his family never cared if he was looking toward them. They only cared if he was listening to them. "I'll tell you this, once I figured out who and what I was and accepted it, I was happier than I'd ever been in my life."

"Yeah?" Robbie felt a glimmer of home spring from deep inside him.

"Absolutely. Geoff told me once that part of being gay is the journey to accept who you are. It's often not an easy journey, but once you make it, you're stronger and happier because of it."

Footsteps in the house signaled the end of their conversation, and Robbie heard Eli get up and begin moving around the room. "You won't say anything to anyone, will you?"

"Of course not, but think about what I said." Robbie felt a light pat on his shoulder and heard Joey walk into the room. "Joey, would you run out to the barn and tell Geoff that dinner will be ready in a few minutes?"

Robbie's phone rang, the now very familiar ringtone signaling another call from his mother. "Hi, Mama." He really didn't feel like talking to her now. What he really wanted was some alone time to think. What he wanted more than anything was some time with his violin. Maybe after dinner he could ask where he could rehearse. "Everything's fine."

"I'm glad, honey. Your father and I are just about to go out, and I wanted to call and make sure you knew where we'd be if you needed us."

"I'm fine, and if I need anything, the people I'm staying with will help me. They're really nice, Mama." He purposely avoided

Love Means ... NO Boundaries

telling her about the farm and Geoff, Eli, and Joey. He knew she'd freak on so many levels. "You don't need to call all the time. I'm fine."

"I don't mind, dear." The woman could be completely oblivious sometimes. "I want to know you're okay." Fine, but calling three times a day is a bit excessive.

"I know, Mama, but I need to go. It's almost time for dinner." He said his goodbyes and hung up the phone as the back door opened.

Dinner was fascinating for Robbie, with everyone talking about what they'd done that day. Joey went on and on about how much help he'd been in the garden, and after dinner, he'd actually taken everyone outside to show them. Robbie loved Joey's enthusiasm. When they came back inside, Robbie asked if there was a place he could rehearse, and Geoff had led him into what he called his office. "You can use this room any time you want. Just close the door and no one will bother you."

Robbie lost track of how long he practiced. Time always seemed to fly when he was playing his violin. His mind filled with music, and he just let it out, let all his emotions, cares, and troubles flow down his arms to his fingers and along the bow until they became part of the instrument, part of the music. When he was exhausted emotionally, he put the wooden extension of himself back in the case along with the bow and gently clasped it shut. Shuffling to the door, he opened it, expecting to hear the television, but he was met with near silence, just the sound of soft breathing.

"That was beautiful, Robbie." Joey's voice seemed choked with emotion, and Robbie wondered if he'd been a little too expressive with his playing, a little too open about his feelings. "Would you like to join us?"

"I think I need to go upstairs. Good night." Robbie thought he knew where he was, but his head was still spinning a little. He felt

Joey's hand on his arm, leading him reassuringly through the house and up the stairs to his room. Robbie put his things away and got ready for bed, climbing between the sheets. As soon as he did, he felt what he thought was a dog jump on the bed.

"Rex, get down from there." Joey's voice scolded the dog lightly from the hallway.

"It's okay. I like it." The dog curled up next to his legs and settled on the covers. He heard Joey say good night and then groan softly, "Lucky dog." Well, that seemed to answer one question for him, but did he have the courage to do anything about it? Did he dare? Did he really want to? In some ways the thought scared him to death, but the more he thought about Joey touching him intimately, the way he touched his arm when he helped him, made him excited and very curious about how it would feel. Lying back in the bed with the dog against his legs, Robbie let his mind wander. If he could see, he'd have been staring at the ceiling, but as it was, he let his mind ponder what Eli had said and eventually fell asleep without any real answers.

CHAPTER 3

"ROBBIE, are you ready for your rehearsal?" Joey finished his coffee and watched as the object of his fascination slowly finished a piece of toast.

"I just need to get my violin."

"I'll get it for you. It's almost nine, and I don't want you to be late." The house was empty except for them. Everyone else was outside, working. Joey retrieved the violin from the office and returned with the case to the kitchen. "Do you think you can make it to the car on your own?"

"I think I can."

"Then I'll follow you." Joey stayed behind and let Robbie make his way to the back door and outside, amazed that Robbie made a direct line toward the car. It hadn't been moved since they'd gotten home the day before, but Robbie's ability to navigate was impressive. "You're amazing, you know that?" Joey commented as he watched Robbie open the passenger door and climb into the car.

"Not really. I've had plenty of practice navigating in the dark," he answered, as Joey handed him the instrument and closed the door before climbing behind the wheel. "I have orchestra rehearsal until eleven, and then we'll have lunch before working with some local music students." Robbie's face lit with excitement. "I love this part. I love working with the kids. In Chattanooga, I got to work with a six-year-old cellist who was blind too. She was having a difficult time, and I was able to help her. After we were done, her mother hugged me and told me she hadn't seen her daughter smile like that in months." Joey glanced at Robbie as he pulled into the drive in front of the auditorium. "Is it okay if I call you when we're done?"

"Of course." Joey gave him the number, and he nimbly programmed it into his phone.

"When we get back, I thought I'd take you to the barn, and you can meet the horses."

"When I was a child, before I got sick, I always wanted a pony, but Mama wouldn't let me get one. I did get to ride one once at a carnival, though."

"Would you like to ride?" Joey wasn't sure how Robbie would feel about it, but he was sure he could get him on a horse and lead him around the yard.

"Could I?" Robbie's face was a study in fascinated wonder.

"Sure." Joey was about to say more when he saw the doors open, and Arie came scuttling toward the car, immediately opening the door.

"Let me help you inside." Arie practically lifted Robbie out of his seat and guided him away from the car like he was some sort of invalid. Joey found himself becoming angry at the way Arie was treating him. Robbie wasn't helpless and most certainly could have made his way inside on his own. Maybe he'd need a little guidance, but he didn't need to be treated like he was useless. Why did Robbie allow it? The car door closed, and Arie glared back at Joey. He began helping Robbie toward the door before letting him go and walking back to the car, rapping on the glass.

Joey lowered the window as Arie peered through the glass and spoke. "We'll bring Robbie back this afternoon."

Joey looked over Arie's shoulder. "You'll call when you're ready?" Robbie smiled in his direction and held up the phone and nodded. Arie saw the gesture and scowled at Joey, but didn't say anything more. Instead he turned and walked back to Robbie, hurrying him inside. *What did I ever do to you?* Then he realized it had happened again. He'd been able to forget until he saw the look on Arie's face, and his fingers went to his face, tracing the pink scars and scowling toward the building as the door swung closed.

Joey pulled away and got to work, spending the day alone, away from the farm and everyone else. At noon he thought about going back to the house for lunch, but couldn't bring himself to be around anyone. He remembered reading the story of the *Hunchback of Notre Dame* in school, and he suddenly realized how Quasimodo might have felt.

As he looked over the hay fields, trying to determine when they might be ready for cutting, he heard the thunder of hooves and saw Eli approaching on Tiger. Pulling up, he slid off the horse's back as gracefully as a ballet dancer. "I brought you some lunch." Eli reached into a saddlebag and brought out a small insulated bag before handing it to Joey along with a thermos. "What's wrong? You look miserable."

Joey shook his head and turned away. "I hate it, Eli. Since the accident, I hate my own face."

"Is it that, or the way others react to you?" Damn, the man was perceptive. "You can't change the way others see you until you change the way you see yourself. You're not broken, Joey, and you're not ugly. The scars have already started to fade and the doctor says that will continue." Eli reached into the other saddlebag and pulled out a second insulated bag. "I can't tell you that you'll look the same as you did before the accident, but regardless, you need to decide if you want to let the way you look define how you see yourself." Joey watched as Eli opened the bag and pulled out a sandwich and took a bite. "I never thought you'd let yourself be measured by how you look." Joey watched as Eli grew quiet and ate quietly.

Slowly, Joey began to move, opening the bag and withdrawing his own food. He didn't feel like eating. "I feel like a fool."

Eli smiled as he swallowed. "You're not a fool, Joey. You've just been feeling sorry for yourself over something as ultimately unimportant as how you look."

"Yeah, I guess." Joey took out a sandwich and began eating, the early summer breeze blowing its cooling breath across the sweet field. "Why didn't you say something earlier?"

"You weren't ready to hear it." Eli's eyes twinkled like he knew something that Joey didn't.

"And you think I am now?"

Eli smiled as he took another bite of his sandwich. "I certainly hope so. I don't know how much more of your moping I can take. Even the horses are starting to get depressed." Eli smiled, and his eyes shone mischievously. "If I have to look at one more horse with a long face...." Eli began to laugh, and Joey couldn't help joining him.

"God, that's a really old joke."

"Yeah, but it got you to laugh didn't it?" Eli continued chuckling as he finished his sandwich and opened his thermos, gulping from the liquid inside.

"Thanks, Eli." Joey finished up the lunch and put the remains back in the bag, handing it to Eli.

Love Means ... NO Boundaries

"You're welcome." Eli closed his lunch kit and put it back in the saddlebag along with Joey's. "I'll see you later." Mounting the horse, Eli waved as he directed Tiger toward home.

Joey watched him leave and felt better than he had in quite some time. Eli was right. He had good friends who cared about him and a mother who would do anything in the world for him. Getting back to work, he spent the rest of the afternoon mapping out his plans for harvesting the first cutting of hay in a few weeks. As he was finishing, his phone rang. It was Robbie telling him he was ready to be picked up. Getting his notes together, he put them in the back seat and began driving.

Pulling up in front of the auditorium, he saw Robbie with Arie waiting next to him, looking impatient and very unhappy. As he pulled up and rolled down the window, he heard Arie complaining that Robbie wouldn't have to wait if he'd just let him bring him back. "That's enough, Arie." Robbie handed Joey his violin and climbed in the car, closing the door. "I'll see you tomorrow for the performance."

"Okay." Joey noticed that Arie's voice became even and happy sounding even as his face glared bullets at Joey. Robbie raised the window and Joey pulled away, doing his best not to look back.

"How'd it go?"

"Really good. The kids were great and so talented. We're going to work with them again in a few days. It's amazing. We work with them four times in two weeks and by the end, you can hear a difference. It's like they're sponges, soaking up everything you say."

"Are you up for meeting some of the horses?"

"Are you kidding? I've been looking forward to that all day." Joey pulled the car into the yard, stopping in front of the barn.

Robbie got out and waited by his closed door. "I can hear them." Joey watched as he turned his head. "That is the horses isn't it?"

"Yup. Let's go inside, and I'll make introductions." Joey led Robbie inside and to the first stall. "This is Belle. She's a sweet old girl." The big head poked out of the stall, and Robbie stepped back as she blew air out her nose. "There's nothing to be afraid of. She just wants to say hello." Joey placed Robbie's hand on her neck so he could stroke her.

"Wow, she's really warm."

"They're heat generators, all right. Belle's basically in retirement. She spends a lot of time in the pastures, and we only ride her occasionally. She loves the kids and is great for their first riding lessons. We don't want to overwork her, but she just loves attention." Belle slid her head against Robbie's chest.

"What's she doing?" There was a slight note of worry in Robbie's voice.

"She's just checking out your pocket, hoping for a treat."

Robbie laughed as Belle rubbed against him. "What's happening outside? It sounds like kids, and they seem to be having fun."

"They are. It's one of Eli's beginner lessons."

"Mr. Joey." A high-pitched, delighted voice called out and small legs ran toward him.

"Karl—oof." Joey's legs were grabbed and hugged as the four-year-old jumped up and down. "How are you, buddy?"

"Good." The youngster's head craned upward. "Who's that?" he pointed toward Robbie as he stood next to Belle still stroking her neck. God, Joey wished he could trade places with that horse. He'd love to have Robbie touching him like that.

Love Means ... NO Boundaries

"That's Mr. Robbie." Joey's legs were released, and Karl walked up to Robbie, lifting his arms to be picked up, but of course Robbie didn't react, he just continued stroking Belle's neck. "He wants you to pick him up." Karl started jumping up and down, his arms still in the air becoming impatient.

"Please, I wanna pet the horsie." Joey walked to Karl and lifted him up, his little hands stroking Belle's neck. "Why can't Mr. Robbie lift me up? Is he hurt?"

"Karl, Mr. Robbie can't see." The look of disbelief on Karl's face was really cute, and it was even cuter when Karl began waving his hands in front of Robbie's face, trying to check out the unbelievable story. Joey couldn't help himself and began to chuckle.

"What's so funny?" Robbie asked, and Joey immediately became serious.

"He's waving his hands in front of your face."

"And that's funny because?" The hurt tone in Robbie's voice cut right to Joey's heart. The last thing he wanted Robbie to think was that he was making fun of him.

"Karl didn't believe me." He set the child back on his feet and scooted him toward the back door where he raced to rejoin the other kids. "I wasn't making fun of you." The very last thing he'd ever do was make fun of anyone. Joey looked into Robbie's sightless eyes and saw that they were filled to overflowing. Without thinking he stepped forward and hugged Robbie to him. "I'm sorry. I thought Karl's reaction was funny. I wasn't laughing at you," he whispered against Robbie's hair as he slightly stroked the smaller man's back. God, Robbie felt good against him, like they fit together. This man drove him to distraction, and holding him like this was like a dream come true. Joey stopped those thoughts cold. What kind of person was he—he'd hurt Robbie, and here he was thinking how hot he made him. "I'd never pick on you that way. I'm sorry."

Joey felt Robbie pull away. "I know. I shouldn't have overreacted."

All he wanted to do was pull him back into his arms and hold him. "You didn't. I think I'd be hurt too."

Robbie's expression softened, and Joey breathed a sigh of relief that he hadn't hurt him too badly. "You said I could go for a ride earlier. Can I still do that?"

Joey smiled involuntarily. Even though Robbie couldn't see it, he smiled at the man. "Of course. Let me get her ready." Joey left Robbie stroking Belle's neck and got her things. It didn't take him long to have her saddled and ready. "Robbie, I'm going to open the stall door. I need you to take a step back and then move about five feet to your left." When Robbie was out of the way, he opened the door and walked Belle outside. "I need you to follow my voice. There's a slight step down about three feet ahead of you." Joey watched every movement Robbie made. "That's it, step down. Good. Now take two more steps. Excellent. Belle is right in front of you." Joey began looking around realizing he had a problem. Normally, he could talk someone through mounting a horse, but Robbie was going to need extra help and he couldn't do it holding Belle's reins. Walking Belle to a fence post, he looped the reins over it and helped Robbie to where Belle stood patiently waiting.

"What do you want me to do?" Robbie stood near the horse.

Joey took Robbie's hand and guided it toward the stirrup, letting him feel it, and he guided his hand to the pommel on the saddle. "Hold on there, and I'll guide your foot into the stirrup, then you stand on that leg, and throw the other one over her back." Joey tapped Robbie's leg. "Lift this foot." He guided it to the stirrup, and he made sure it was inside. "Now lift your body, and I'll help guide your leg over." Robbie stood up in the stirrup. "Excellent, now bring your leg up and over." Joey steadied Robbie's body as he brought his leg over the horse before settling into the saddle. "You did great. How does it feel?"

"Different."

"I'm sure it does. Let me adjust the stirrups, and then I'll lead you around the yard. Your body will sway with the movement of the horse, and I want you to tell me if you feel uncomfortable. I'll have the reins, so I just want you to have fun."

Robbie suddenly looked concerned. "What if I fall?"

"If you feel like you're going to fall off, stay loose and roll when you feel the ground, but you shouldn't have a problem." Taking the reins, Joey patted Belle's neck. "I'm going to turn the horse, and then we'll begin walking." Leading Belle around, he began walking across the farmyard.

Cars began pulling into the yard, parents picking up their kids from their lesson, so Joey walked Belle and Robbie around the house. "You doing okay?"

"Okay?" Joey looked back and saw an ear-to-ear grin on Robbie's face. "This is amazing." Joey watched as Robbie got a pair of sunglasses out of his shirt pocket and slipped them on.

"Why the sunglasses?" Joey continued leading them around the yard. It didn't really matter where they were going. From the look on his face, Robbie was having a spectacular time.

"My eyes themselves are fine; it's the nerves that are bad. Since I can't see the sun, I could look into it and burn my eyes, which would be painful. So I wear sunglasses to protect them, like everyone else."

Joey continued walking. "I never thought of that." They walked in silence for a while, Robbie holding the pommel. "You can hold her mane if you need to; it won't hurt her. If you want more stability, grip her with your legs and thighs."

They walked around the yard for an hour, Robbie's smile remaining in place the entire time. "How long can I ride?" Robbie was loving this; it was plain for anyone to see.

"We should head in. I don't want your legs to hurt. Do you think you can get down on your own?"

"I think so." Robbie looked thoroughly happy, his smile bright and huge. Joey found himself wondering what those lips would feel like next to his, what they'd taste like.

Joey stopped the horse on the grass. "Hold onto the pommel and slip your left foot out of the stirrup. Good. Now stand on your right leg and bring your left foot over her back and down to the ground. It's a ways down, so don't let go until your foot is on the ground." Robbie slipped his foot out of the stirrup and stood up, his leg going over the horse. "Excellent, now bend your knee and lower your foot to the ground." Joey watched every move. "That's it, a little more. Good, now slip your right foot out of the stirrup, and you're standing on the ground."

"What do I do now?"

"Just step back, and I'll get Belle in her stall and come back for you." He took a few steps and stopped. "You looked great on her, like you belonged there." Actually, Joey thought Robbie would look great anywhere, especially in his bed. Joey walked Belle back to her stall and raced back to Robbie before leading him back to the barn with Robbie smiling and laughing the entire time. Each smile, each chuckle, went right to Joey's heart, and he knew he'd do a lot to put that smile on Robbie's face again.

As they entered, a number of majestic heads appeared, and Robbie veered off to the side. "Who's this?" He pointed to the horse breathing heavily near him.

"That's Tiger, Eli's horse. He's very friendly, but don't get too close. He's a little energetic." Joey stepped to Robbie, about to guide him away when Tiger thumped his head against Robbie's chest, and Joey could only watch as Robbie lost his balance. He saw him step backward and stumble before falling backward. Joey tried to react, but watched as his body collapsed backward, his head hitting the concrete.

HE HATED falling. His body tensed, and he had no idea when it would stop. All his references failed him, and he felt completely helpless. He heard Joey call to him, but couldn't do anything.

The next thing he remembered, Joey's arms were around his body, and he was helping him sit up. "Robbie, are you okay?"

"Yes." His head hurt, and he rubbed it, his fingers coming back wet. "I must have cut myself."

"Can you sit up?" Robbie nodded his head slowly, and then Joey's hands were gone, and he heard footsteps hurry away. Then the footsteps returned and a warm cloth pressed to his head. "Let me help you get cleaned up." Joey's voice was soft and heavy, like he was scared and worried. Joey's touch was so gentle and soft. The cloth moved away, and he felt fingers probe his hair. "It's not large and the bleeding seems to be stopping." The cloth pressed to his head again, and Joey got quiet for a while. "I'm sorry, Robbie."

He heard other footsteps in the barn and recognized Geoff's voice as he asked what happened. "I fell."

"It was my fault." Joey sounded guilty.

"No, it wasn't. I fell. It's not the first time, and it won't be the last." Robbie began to get to his feet.

"What happened?" Arie's voice filled the barn as footsteps rushed in his direction.

"I'm fine, Arie, I just fell."

"What was he doing in here? He could get hurt, did get hurt." Robbie didn't like the accusatory tone in Arie's voice. His fall wasn't anyone's fault.

"Arie, I'm fine!"

"Weren't you watching him?" The judgmental tone in Arie's voice grated Robbie the wrong way. "Did you leave him alone?"

"That's enough, Arie! It wasn't Joey's fault. I fell, it happens, get over yourself."

"They're supposed to look out for you." The accusatory tone was gone from Arie's voice, switched off and replaced with a soothing, smooth tone. "Let's get you out of here."

Robbie shrugged away. "I'm fine, Arie." Robbie regained his balance. "What are you doing here anyway?" He felt Joey's hand on his arm. He'd know that touch anywhere.

"I just stopped by to see how you were doing. I know it can take a while for you to learn new places, and I wanted to see if you needed help getting ready for the performance tonight.

"You didn't need to come all that way. I'm fine, and any help I need Joey can handle." He couldn't believe how angry he was with Arie. He had no right to come in here and take over, telling everyone what to do. He wasn't helpless, and he particularly resented the way Arie treated Joey. It wasn't his fault that he'd fallen. He wanted to lash out, but controlled himself. "I'll meet you at the auditorium later."

Robbie heard Arie's heavy footsteps and assumed he was storming off. "Did he look mad?" They began walking out of the barn, back toward the house.

"Uh, yeah. If looks could kill, I'd be dead right now."

"Arie," Robbie shook his head. "He's as gentle as a kitten."

Love Means ... NO Boundaries

He felt a tenseness in Joey's muscles that wasn't there before, and he wondered what caused it, but Joey said nothing as they continued walking.

"Step up into the house."

"Hey, boys, dinner is almost ready." Dishes clanked as he heard Eli working. "Looks like you took a tumble." He felt Eli guide him to a chair and begin fussing over him, washing the cut and making sure he was truly fine. "It's only a really small cut." Then his fingers slipped away. "When do you need to be at the auditorium?"

"The concert's at eight, so I need to be there at seven-thirty."

"We'll drive you over, and I got tickets for all of us."

"Excellent." He heard the pleasure in Geoff's voice. From the soft, fabric-muffled sounds, he figured he was setting the table.

"Do you need your cane?" Joey asked.

Robbie nodded and felt the familiar object press into his hand. Knowing his way much better now, he walked to the bathroom, closing the door behind him. It felt like he'd been in the house a lot longer than just a few days. In his mind, he knew where everything was. It was like this house, this farm, felt comfortable, right. Washing and drying his hands, he opened the door and walked back to the table, sitting in the same chair he'd used the day before.

He heard when a plate was set down in front of him and Joey explained where and what everything was. Fried chicken and small potatoes. Robbie smiled to himself as he began eating slowly.

He'd noticed that after the first dinner, meals had consisted almost exclusively of finger foods. No one had said anything, but he'd noticed it happening just the same. Even breakfast had morphed into egg sandwiches on toast. They hadn't said anything—

and he didn't either—but silently, he said a "thank you" to Eli and his new friends for their thoughtful kindness.

After dinner, he was shooed upstairs to get ready. Robbie noticed something else as he walked up the stairs—he had a shadow that he assumed was Rex. Opening his bedroom door, he heard the bed squeak slightly as Rex jumped on the bed, followed by panting. He reached out and stroked the soft creature. "You're a good boy, aren't you?" A wet tongue licked his fingers and hand. "You want to keep me company?" He felt the dog's tongue on his face and stroked the dog's hair. It felt so good on his skin. He'd always wanted a dog, but his mother was allergic.

Moving to the closet, he located his tuxedo and laid it on the bed before sliding off his shoes and socks and then lowering his pants. Robbie stepped into his tuxedo pants. The cool, crisp material felt good on his legs as he slid them on. Taking off his T-shirt, he laid it next to his pants and felt around inside the bag looking for his dress shirt but couldn't find it.

"I think you have a friend for life." Robbie jumped when he heard Joey's voice, not expecting him since he hadn't heard his footsteps.

He heard a soft gasp, but didn't know what it was for. "Is something wrong?"

"N-no." The stammer just confused him more.

"Then why are you breathing funny and stammering?"

"You're beautiful." Joey's breathy words took him by surprise.

"I'm what?" Robbie could barely believe his ears.

"Um." Robbie waited, hoping Joey would repeat the words he could barely believe he'd heard. "I said you're beautiful." Then nothing, and Robbie wondered if that admission meant what he thought it meant. His body sure hoped it did. "I'm sorry. I shouldn't have…." He heard Joey's voice trail off and retreating footsteps.

Love Means ... NO Boundaries

"Joey." The footsteps stopped. "I didn't say I was upset." He let his hands fall to his side, his attention tuned to the last footsteps he'd heard and waited for what seemed like an eternity. Most of the time he'd accepted the fact that he couldn't see, but there were times, like right now, that he very much wished he could. He wanted to see Joey's expression, look into his eyes. Maybe have a clue what he was thinking. But all he could do was wait and listen to his breathing and Rex's panting from the bed. It was unnerving. "Am I really beautiful?" He'd never really wondered what he looked like. Since he couldn't see, it wasn't really important to him. But it suddenly seemed very important.

"Yes." He heard the whisper, but no footsteps followed. "Really beautiful." Then a soft step reached his ears, followed by another.

He felt the heat from Joey's body. Was he going to kiss him? What would it be like? His body was ready to push him forward, but he waited, wondering.

Fingertips caressed his cheek and a thumb ghosted over his upper lip. He gasped and the touch retreated.

"I'm sorry."

Robbie stepped forward. "Nothing to be sorry for, except maybe pulling away." He reached out to Joey, his hands encountering a warm shirt, hard muscle beneath.

"You gasped."

"It was that good." If it was possible to hear someone smile, Robbie did at that moment. The touch was back, fingers sliding over his cheek. Robbie didn't know what to do, so he stayed still, afraid Joey would stop what he was doing. Then he felt a soft pressure on his lips, gentle and hot. He wasn't sure it was really there.

The pressure increased, and he knew it for what it was: his first real kiss. And he responded, with gusto. Lifting his arms, he entwined them around Joey's body as the kiss deepened.

Robbie's mind began to swirl with every emotion imaginable, and his body felt like it was on fire. If this was what it meant to be gay—bring it on, and the world be damned. His mind cleared just enough that he could feel Joey's hands sliding over his chest and around to his bare back.

"Robbie."

"Don't stop." If he stopped, then this would be over, and he didn't want it to end. He felt Joey's lips soften and pull away, but he could still feel his hot breath on his skin and hear soft panting that mirrored his own.

"I can't do this to you. You're beautiful and I'm…."

"You're what?"

"I'm so ugly."

Robbie raised his hands to Joey's face and felt smooth skin, then wetness. He ran his hand over Joey's cheek and back through his hair. "You feel beautiful to me."

He heard Joey's breath hitch and a soft sniffle. His lips were taken again as fingers wound their way through his hair. He wanted… for the first time in his life, he knew what it felt like to want another person so badly he'd rather give up breathing than stop kissing.

"Robbie, we need to leave soon." Eli's voice calling up the stairs broke them out of their desire-induced daze. Joey kissed him one last time and stepped away.

"I need my shirt and can't find it."

Love Means ... NO Boundaries

He heard Joey begin looking through his closet. "I don't know. I think you'd be the talk of the evening if you went without one." He heard Joey chuckle.

"It'd be a little nipply... I mean nippy." He chuckled as well as his shirt was placed in his hand. Robbie slipped it on, and he shivered as Joey helped him with his cufflinks, fingers lingering on his hand.

"Here's your tie and jacket."

Robbie put them on and sat on the edge of the bed, Rex scooting closer for a scratch. "Are my socks the right color? I once wore white socks to a performance. Can you say 'Which violinist is blind?'"

"Your socks are fine." Joey continued chuckling.

Robbie slipped on his shoes and felt Joey kiss him again. "I need to get ready too. I'll be right back."

He heard Joey leave the room and got up to begin making his way downstairs when his mama alarm went off again. "I'm getting ready for a performance, and I have to leave soon. Can I call you later?"

"I just called to wish you a good performance and to make sure everything was okay."

"Everything's fine, Mama." He couldn't keep some of his exasperation out of his voice. Her three times a day calls were starting to get on his nerves. After all, he wasn't a child. "I'll call you later. I don't want to be late." Their calls were becoming shorter and shorter. There was never anything new to tell her because she called too often.

He heard a soft beeping on the line. "Okay, honey." Now she was in a hurry because she had another call. Hanging up the phone, he turned it off and slipped it in his pocket as he heard footsteps approach the room.

"Shall we go?" Joey's hand touched his arm, and he could immediately feel the heat through his shirt and jacket.

Carrying his cane, he let Joey lead him to Geoff's large car, climbing in what he assumed was the back seat. Doors closed, and his violin was placed on his lap just before he felt the car begin to move. Voices and conversation swirled around him as they rode the short distance.

The car stopped moving, and Robbie heard car doors opening and felt a now familiar hand on his arm.

"I'll help you inside." Arie's voice rang in his ears, and Robbie wanted so badly to tell him that Joey could do it, but practical concerns won out. He and Arie were going to the same place, after all.

Going with Arie, he followed his friend's instructions silently, wishing that it was Joey's hand on his arm and his voice in his ear. Reaching the backstage area, he sat down his case and got out his instrument, tuned it, and sat down to wait. Arie sat next to him like he usually did, talking about the music and whatnot. Robbie barely listened. He was still angry with Arie, but he knew his friend was just concerned about him. He turned to him and almost opened his mouth to apologize, but stopped himself. He wasn't going to say he was sorry for standing up for himself. "We should go."

The words cut through Robbie's thoughts, and he got to his feet and followed Arie out front.

He could feel the heat from the lights as he walked out the door onto the stage. "Thank you." He received a reassuring touch and sat down. Whispers and the din of overlapping conversations met his ears, but he tuned them out as he listened for a particular voice, a certain timbre. And he heard it, cutting through the other sounds like a ringing bell, drawing his attention. He turned and smiled, hoping Joey knew it was for him.

The audience applauded and the concert master tuned the orchestra, in a cacophony of planned aural chaos. The room became quiet again, followed by more applause as the conductor stepped out on the stage.

Robbie felt his footsteps across the stage, and then a familiar soft tap signaled all was ready. Then came an equally familiar vibration as the conductor tapped his foot setting the time.

The first note carried Robbie on a journey as he drew the bow across the strings. Music always carried him away, filled his acute senses with beauty. He played like he'd never played before. The blood surged through his veins, his ears full of the sounds of the other musicians, their efforts heightening his own. The auditorium may have been full of people, but he played for just one. His fingers flowed nimbly over the strings, his bow an extension of his hand, the music an amplification of his voice and emotions, sending his joy to Joey.

All too quickly, the music came to an end. The applause rolled over him as his full heart pounded in his chest, fueled by the adrenaline of performing. A tap on his shoulder signaled him, and Robbie stood and bowed.

Heady from the performance, he made his way back stage and gathered his things together. His violin and bow went back in their protective case, and he waited for Joey, Eli, and Geoff. Then his phone rang.

"Hi, Mama." His excitement extended to her call. "The performance was great."

"I'm glad." She sounded off, upset.

"Why didn't you tell me you were staying on a farm? I found out from Arie that you fell and hurt yourself." Now Arie was acting as his mother's spy.

"Mama, it was nothing. I just lost my balance, I'm fine."

"Not a farm with all those animals and huge, sharp pieces of equipment." Her voice was just dripping with worry.

"Mama, I'm just fine," he reiterated, as he thought of killing Arie. "You don't need to worry."

"I know. I worked it out with the lovely people Arie's staying with. They're going to take you as well."

"What?" Robbie felt like someone had punched him in the stomach.

"Arie will be able to help you and watch over you to make sure you're okay."

"I don't need a babysitter." He knew he was talking loudly and that others could hear him, but he was too upset to care.

"Well, you need someone. When Arie told me you'd fallen in a barn and were bleeding, I almost got on a plane myself." Her voice was becoming more frantic. "So you go back to that farm, and Arie will help you pack your things. Tell them thank you and all, but it's just not safe."

Robbie's first reaction was to go along with her—she knew best, she always had. Whether it was his Southern upbringing or the fact that she'd taken special care of him for the last ten years, he almost went along. He felt almost helpless to do anything else. But he liked the farm and his new friends. He liked the fact that they encouraged him to do things on his own. He'd done things on the farm his mother would never have allowed. And most of all, he'd miss his chances with Joey.

"Mother, would you listen to yourself? I'm not helpless." Why did he seem to be saying this so often lately? He didn't want to leave the farm, but he wasn't ready to tell her the real reason why. He couldn't tell her that he liked Joey and was finally figuring out what it meant to be gay. He'd never talked about any of this with either of his parents, and he knew he didn't want to tell her over the phone.

Joey... if he were honest with himself, the real reason he didn't want to leave was him. He wanted to know what it would be like to kiss him again, maybe do more than kiss, but he wasn't going to get that chance if he had to leave. "I like it on the farm. They make me feel useful." He could hear that she was gearing up to say something else. "Yes, Mama, useful. I helped plant a garden and got to ride a horse. They don't treat me like I'm broken."

"Honey, you're not broken."

"I know, Mama, but everyone treats me like I am, including you." He heard a sharp intake of breath come through the phone.

"No I don't."

"You just did." The line went quiet. "You decided what was best for your adult son without even asking me." Robbie lowered his voice as more people entered the room. "You didn't ask or discuss it with me, you just decided."

"I was worried about you."

"I know you were, but I can't have you doing things like that."

"I'm your mother, and I worry."

"I know, but I'm fine, and I like it here. I even have a dog that sleeps on my bed at night." He didn't say who else he hoped he'd have in his bed—he didn't want her to have a stroke.

He waited for his mother and the line was silent for a while. "You'll tell Arie?"

Robbie knew he'd won, at least this round, and decided to go for broke. "No, you will. My ride is waiting for me, and I have to go." After saying goodbye, he breathed a sigh of relief and hung up the phone.

"Did you talk to your mom?" Arie asked as his phone rang.

"Yes. You should get that." He'd let his mother tell him.

A hand rested on his arm, and he felt a hot tingle through his body. "Are you ready?"

"Yes."

"I've got your violin," Joey said as Robbie got his cane, and Joey led him to the car. The tingles only increased, and Robbie wondered if that feeling would continue when Joey touched him in other places.

The ride to the farm was quick, with everyone telling him how much they liked the performance. "We don't get many things like that here," Geoff said from the driver's seat. "It's very special. Do you keep performing the same things?"

"Yes and no. Our next performance will be the same, but the final two performances will be Beethoven's ninth with local soloists and choir. Audiences always love the 'Ode to Joy'." Geoff pulled into the drive, and Robbie made his way into the house with Joey's help.

"Would anyone like something to eat before bed?" Eli asked as they entered the kitchen.

"No, thank you." Robbie actually yawned, the excitement from the performance waning. "I think I'll head to bed. Good night," Robbie said, carrying his instrument with him.

Rex, who had sneaked inside when they got home, followed Robbie up the stairs and jumped on the bed when Robbie opened the bedroom door.

Getting cleaned up, he walked back to the room wearing only his pants and bumped into Joey, who said nothing and kissed him.

Love Means ... NO Boundaries

The door closed and Robbie felt himself being maneuvered toward the bed. Strong, work-hardened arms and hands lowered him to the bed. "Joey?"

He felt Joey's bare chest press to his as lips devoured him. His entire body was overwhelmed by the same tingles of excitement he'd felt earlier from Joey's simple touch. "Are we?" His question ended with another kiss; then the lips drew away, and he imagined Joey looking down at him. "Please talk to me."

"I want... I just can't." What kind of answer was that? Then the lips were back and Robbie felt the passion increase. Letting his hands roam, he felt strong muscles and impressive shoulders flow beneath his hands. Robbie wanted out of these clothes, but Joey made no effort to remove them, he just kept kissing him within an inch of his life. He gave up on speech and moaned softly as the erotic assault continued.

Abruptly, the kissing stopped, and he felt Joey's weight lift from him. "I... how can you.... Good night, Robbie," Joey stuttered.

Before he could respond or reply, he heard footsteps and then a door closing. Robbie touched his lips with his fingers. He could still feel them singing from Joey's kisses. "What happened?"

He didn't know the answer, but he sure as hell was going to find out. He almost got up and marched into Joey's bedroom to ask him, but he had a lot of thinking to do. Getting undressed, he hung up his clothes and crawled beneath the covers, feeling Rex sneak nearer. "At least I have you for company." His body throbbed with arousal as he settled in the bed and thought about taking care of things himself, but didn't. Instead he did his best to calm his mind so he could sleep. Joey's reaction was completely confusing. Robbie knew Joey had been aroused, and it was sexy that he could get him that excited, but the reaction was almost weird. "What the hell happened?"

CHAPTER 4

JOEY made it back to his room and closed the door before collapsing against it. He'd practically assaulted the man. How could he do that to Robbie? He'd gotten lost in the feel of his lips until he'd seen his reflection in the closet mirror. Then he remembered and had to get out. Robbie deserved better than him. Yes, he was blind, but he deserved someone who wouldn't have everyone he met cringing. He really liked Robbie, maybe more than liked him. Was he scared? God, was he ever. He could fall for Robbie and fall hard, but Robbie was going to leave.

"I'm so confused," he said to the room as he pushed away from the door. "What must Robbie be thinking?" He banged his head against the door and left it there. "I'm such an idiot." He finally pushed away and began getting ready for bed. He almost went to Robbie's room to try to explain, but he didn't even have an explanation for himself, let alone for Robbie. Climbing between the sheets, he turned off the light and stared at the ceiling, the berating voice in his head not letting him sleep.

Joey must have slept a little because he woke to a strange sound in the house. Opening his bedroom door, he noticed that

Love Means ... NO Boundaries

Robbie's was open as well. Geoff and Eli's door remained closed. Following the sound, he padded down the stairs and the sound, while still muffled, grew louder and appeared to be coming from Geoff's office. Approaching the door, he could hear it clearly now. It was Robbie's violin.

The music was slow, almost mournful, and it reached into Joey's gut and twisted. He knew what emotion Robbie was playing, because he'd felt the same thing. He could hear all the confusion and insecurity that Robbie must have felt when he left him so abruptly. The playing stopped, and Joey stood still, not making a sound. Then it resumed, the long, low notes searing into Joey's emotions. He could feel every bit of Robbie's confusion and sadness in each note he played.

He stepped forward, standing right next to the door, and raised his hand to knock but stopped. The berating voice in his head started again, calling him a coward, and with a deep breath, he gently rapped on the door. "Robbie, it's me." He opened the door and saw Robbie standing in the office wearing only a pair of white briefs, holding the violin by its neck. As he turned to look at him, he saw on Robbie's face all the emotion he'd heard in the music.

"I didn't mean to wake you."

"You didn't. I haven't slept."

"That makes two of us." Joey watched as Robbie placed the instrument back in its case. "Why'd you leave?"

"I…. It's hard to explain."

Robbie closed the case and picked it up by the handle and slowly walked to the doorway, standing toe to toe with Joey. "Do you want to try?"

Joey nodded on reflex and whispered, "Okay."

Robbie didn't move. "I'm staying here until you explain why you treated me that way."

Joey tried to get his thoughts together so he could explain. "I-I know you can't see me, but if you did, you wouldn't want anything to do with me." Joey felt like a coward.

"Not that again. What's the real reason? What's got you so scared?" For being blind, Robbie saw things pretty well. "I can hear it in your voice."

"I guess I'm…." Joey tried to explain but stopped when he felt Robbie's fingers on his face. They slid over his forehead and around his eyes, over his cheeks and along his jaw line. Everywhere they touched he could feel his skin come alive. The fingers wound through his hair and caressed his ears, making him giggle softly.

"Are you worried about these lines? They're healing. I can feel how you flinch whenever I touch them." A finger ran down the scar on his right cheek. "These aren't you, and they don't make you ugly. They just are." The fingers ran along his lips and without thinking, Joey kissed them as they passed. "Joey, I'm blind. My entire world is black. I live through touch." He ran his finger under Joey's chin. "Scent." He brought his nose hear Joey's neck, inhaling deeply. "Sound." Robbie rested an ear against Joey's chest. "And taste." His head lifted, and he touched his lips to Joey's. "What something looks like doesn't matter to me."

Tears welled in Joey's eyes and fell down his cheek. Robbie's fingers brushed through it, and he brought the finger to his lips. "I'm sorry I hurt you," Joey said, taking Robbie's hands in his, holding them tight as he looked into those big, blue, sightless eyes. It didn't matter to Joey that they couldn't see. Those eyes were still beautiful. Taking a step back, he held Robbie's hand and slowly led him upstairs.

"Where are you taking me?" Robbie suddenly sounded so tentative.

Love Means ... NO Boundaries

"To your room."

"Oh." Robbie sounded disappointed until Joey led him in the room and shut the door. "You're staying?" Joey saw the hopeful look on Robbie's face as he turned toward him.

"If you'll let me." Joey felt Robbie's hands on him, and then he was being hugged and finally kissed. Slowly he lowered Robbie onto the bed. Robbie kept kissing him, and he returned it, tasting his sweet lips, his tongue exploring.

"What do I do?"

Joey could see nothing, only hear. "Have you ever… before?"

"No." He could hear the embarrassment in Robbie's voice. "There was someone at home who seemed interested, but…."

"We'll take it slow." Joey pulled Robbie into his arms, kissing him deeply, pressing their bodies together. He could feel Robbie's excitement against his skin.

Robbie's head rested on the pillow as Joey made sure he was comfortable. After placing another kiss on those incredible lips, he began kissing his way down Robbie's body, hot sweet skin passing under his lips. He wanted Robbie, all of him. He smiled against his skin as Robbie arched and writhed beneath his kisses. "Is it supposed to feel like this?"

"Is it good?"

"Yes, very good."

"Then that's exactly how it's supposed to feel." Joey swirled his tongue around a taut nipple and Robbie cried out softly, arching into the touch.

"Joey." Robbie cried out softly as he continued working the firm bud. Joey let his hands wander over Robbie's skin, palms sliding down his side, over his chest, and along his smooth stomach. He wanted to feel every inch of this man, needed to feel his

61

beautiful body against his skin. Joey wanted everything all at once. Like a starving man looking for food, he wanted every inch of Robbie, and he wanted it now. Bringing their lips together again, he lowered himself onto Robbie and felt his arms pull him closer. Robbie's hands slid along his back as they kissed and kissed. "Joey," Robbie began panting and thrusting against him, pressing their hips together hard.

He knew by Robbie's breathing and his erratic movement that Robbie was close. He wanted to see him, but it was so dark. Instead he reveled in the small sounds and whimpers as Robbie softly cried out his pleasure. Joey smiled, climaxing right behind him, neither of them having taken off their underwear. Slowly, Joey got up and helped Joey out of his briefs, wiping him gently before slipping out of his own.

Climbing into the bed, he hugged Robbie to him, kissing him. A thump and prancing feet signaled that Rex had joined them on the bed. Joey heard Robbie giggle against his skin. "He stands guard against the monsters." Robbie turned in Joey's embrace, resting his head against Joey's shoulder as he tried in vain to stifle a yawn. "Good night, Joey." He felt Robbie snuggle against him, and soon his breathing evened out as he drifted off to sleep, and Joey followed quickly behind him.

Joey woke as a hand landed on his face and then moved away. Robbie was tossing around, making small noises, and Joey wondered what he was dreaming about. He didn't seem to be having a nightmare. Soon, Robbie settled back on the mattress, never waking. Over the past two days, Joey had watched Robbie a lot, but this was special. The man was beautiful while he slept. The room had warmed when the morning sun hit the house, and Robbie had pushed down the covers until they were just above those slender hips.

Gently, Joey let his hand slide along the bone, fingers ghosting over the soft skin, tracing the line that led from the exposed waist until the blanket cut off his route. Unlike last night he could see now. He could see the smooth, honey-colored skin, the small nipples that perked when Joey breathed on them, and Robbie's chin covered with the barest beginnings of a dark beard.

Flopping again, Robbie rolled on the bed, the blanket slipping down farther and now covering only his legs as he hugged the pillow, his smooth butt open to appreciative eyes.

Joey couldn't resist, his hand sliding down into the small of Robbie's back and then over the perfect curves to the edge of the blanket.

Footsteps in the hallway broke him out of his deliciously erotic thoughts. He'd like nothing better than to stay in bed, but there was work to be done. So he carefully got out of bed and then leaned over and kissed Robbie softly on the cheek, nuzzling his lips against his soft neck.

"Hmm." Robbie's eyes didn't open, but his head turned into the sensation.

"Sleep. I have to get to work."

He heard another soft noise from Robbie and then felt a closed-eyed kiss on his cheek. Satisfied, Joey got up and poked his head out the door. The hall was now empty, and he dashed across the hall as he heard the door to Geoff and Eli's room open. He hoped he'd gotten inside before either Geoff or Eli got a glimpse of his bare behind.

Dressing quickly, he bounded down the stairs to where Eli and Geoff were seated at the table, each with a cup of coffee and a sleepy look. "Rough night?" Joey grinned as he poured himself a cup. Turning around he saw Geoff smirk at his lover. The shared look was enough to tell Joey that they'd been heard.

"What's on the agenda for today?" Joey asked before sipping from his mug and bringing it to the table.

"The guys are going to check out a few of the pastures, make sure they're clear of things that'll hurt the cattle before we open them up. How about you?"

Joey tried to stifle a yawn and failed. "I've got a few fields to check on, and I promised the guys I'd help check out some of the fence in the south pastures."

Geoff nodded his agreement. "Got to get the books up to date, and I've got an appointment at the bank." He turned to his lover. "Do you have a class?"

"Yeah. I've got a class late this morning and three private lessons this afternoon."

"Well, we should get started." Geoff pushed back his chair and walked with his mug through the house to his office, disappearing inside. Geoff was an accountant, and it still took him a lot of time to keep the books of an enterprise of this size and scale up to date.

Joey got up and put his cup in the sink, looking through the house to the stairs.

Eli seemed to read his mind. "Don't worry. I'll be here when he gets up."

Joey nodded and left the kitchen, going to one of the farm trucks. A few hours later, the last of the fields inspected and checked, he pointed the truck back toward the farm.

Walking inside, he found Eli and Robbie in the kitchen. Robbie stood at the counter, up to his elbows in bread dough, grinning from ear to ear. "Is that you, Joey?"

"Yup." Joey chuckled. "You're covered in flour." Robbie shrugged and kept working the dough.

"Is that good?" Robbie asked Eli.

Love Means ... NO Boundaries

Eli checked the texture. "Sure is, now form the dough into two equal hunks and place them in the bowls. There's one to the left and one to the right." Eli went back to work, letting Robbie finish up.

Joey almost asked Robbie if he needed help, but stopped. Robbie would ask if he did. "I was wondering if you're feeling adventurous."

Robbie split the dough and held a hunk in each hand, balancing the weight. Setting them down, he located the bowls and placed the dough in each. "What did you have in mind?" Eli handed him two towels, and he set the bowls aside carefully and covered each one. The movements were slow and methodical but accomplished with confidence.

"I need to check on some fences, and I was wondering if you'd like to go with me. I can saddle Twilight, and you could ride with me."

"You mean really ride, like behind you?"

"Yeah, if you want."

Robbie really seemed to like the idea, smiling and nodding.

"Then let's get you cleaned up, and we'll get going. Can you find your way to the barn or do you need help?"

Eli spoke up. "You get the horse saddled, and I'll bring Robbie out when he's ready."

Joey touched Robbie's shoulder and went to the barn whistling happily. Inside, he brushed Twilight and got her saddled and ready. He was tightening the girth as he heard Eli and Robbie enter the barn.

"You met Tiger yesterday." Eli told Robbie. "This is Kirk, he's a headstrong one, but it's all just show." Joey peeked out and saw Eli feeding the midnight stallion a few carrots. "This is Belle, short for Tinkerbelle. She's great with the kids and loves attention."

Joey went back to work, listening as Eli continued showing Robbie around. He knew that noses and necks were being petted and scratched. A few times he heard Robbie laugh and croon at the big babies. The man may not be able to see, but he saw better than most people, and he had no fear or guile. The horses loved him for that.

That's when it hit him: Robbie trusted them. He tried to imagine not being able to see, always reliant on what others told him or showed him, clues to reality and deception coming only from sound or the slight inflection in other's voices. Hell, Robbie was about to trust him while they were both on the back of a half-ton animal. What a responsibility and turn-on at the same time. The level of trust was incredibly sexy, and his pants got tight thinking about it. He actually had to think unsexy thoughts to get things to go down.

He continued getting Twilight ready and heard Robbie's phone ring. He shook his head when he heard the now familiar electronic tune. Robbie's voice droned softly as Joey finished saddling Twilight. As he finished, Robbie hung up. "Are you ready?"

Robbie's excitement rang through the barn. "You bet!"

"I'll meet you two out front."

When Joey brought Twilight around, he saw Robbie bending down, Rex jumping for some attention. "Hey, boy."

"Let's me get on first, and Eli will help you." Joey mounted and scooted forward, slipping his feet out of the stirrups. Robbie mounted behind him. "Put your arms around my waist and scoot close to me." Thank goodness they were both thin. The saddle was tight, but at least the pommel wasn't pressing against his bits.

He felt Robbie's arms slink around his waist, hips pressed against his butt, thighs against the back of his legs. "Have fun, you two. And call if you find anything, and I'll send someone out. Lumpy and Pete are just itching to mend fences." The sarcasm was almost funny. It was the one chore those two men hated above all else.

Clicking his teeth, he bumped Twilight's side and she began walking across the yard. "We'll head out across one of the fields and then down a wooded path to the south pastures. I'll let you know to duck if we encounter any low branches."

"Okay. What should I do?" They rode quietly across the field.

"Just enjoy the ride. Are your sunglasses on?"

He felt Robbie's chuckle. "Yes, mother."

Joey returned the laughter. "I'm not that bad."

"No one's that bad. She always worries, but she's called me three or four times a day since I left on the tour. I thought I was going to be away from her for a while. Boy, was I wrong."

"My mother's in Florida, and she still calls me and asks if I'm okay and eating right. I think my mom's a little lonely."

"Maybe that's what's got mine as well. Papa works, but Mama always stayed home, managed the house and grounds, and took care of me."

"It was hard for my mom when I went away to college, but she adapted." Joey laughed. "And drove me crazy whenever I came home. I thought she was going to smother me."

"I'm sure mine will when I get home. She's already trying, but things won't be the same. I've already done more things for myself here than I ever do at home."

"Huh?"

"Mama would never let me help in the gardens. I might get hurt. If she saw me right now, she'd have a heart attack." Joey felt Robbie rest his head against his shoulder, the warmth seeping through his shirt. "I've never helped in the kitchen before. When Eli asked me if I wanted to help him make bread, I thought he was nuts." The words sounded wonderful as Robbie's heavy Southern accent snuck into his speech. "But I had a great time, and I was able to help."

"If you don't help at home, what do you do?"

"Read. I've got tons of books in Braille, and I play and rehearse. Sometimes I just listen to the radio and stuff. Half the time when I leave my room, someone's offering to help me get whatever I need or go wherever I need to go. I know that house like the back of my hand and almost no one lets me find my own way around. Either Mama's helping me or one of the housekeepers is escorting me where I need to go." Joey felt Robbie tip backward slightly. "I love this. The feel of the horse under me, the sun, the breeze." Robbie laughed a little before inhaling deeply. "It smells so fresh. No exhaust fumes or people, just fresh and clean." Joey wished he could turn around and see the smile he felt sure graced Robbie's face. Smiling to himself, he guided Twilight forward.

They approached the woods, and Joey stopped the horse. "Housekeeper? How big is this place?"

"Big. At least I remember it as big. It had columns and a huge porch out front. It's been in daddy's family since before the war."

Joey whistled at Robbie's description. "You mean it's an antebellum plantation?"

"Yes. Mama revels in historic preservation, meaning spending Papa's money, and Papa revels in making it. We're a good, old-fashioned Southern family." Robbie's accent became very pronounced, and Joey laughed at the affectation.

"We're about to enter the woods. We'll take it slow in case we come on any low branches." Joey turned around to check on Robbie and saw Rex loping across the field, heading in their direction. "We're being followed."

"Followed by who?"

Love Means ... No Boundaries

"Rex. I think he wants to keep an eye on you." They started moving forward again, the horse and riders entering the trees. The shade felt coolingly glorious, and the slight breeze was lovely, but did nothing to cool Joey's thoughts. He was acutely aware of Robbie behind him, his arms, his hands, and the way his pelvis ground against his butt. His... was that what he thought it was? Joey shifted back slightly. Yup. He smiled as he felt Robbie's hardness press against him. "I take it riding makes you horny."

"You make me horny," Robbie snickered softly.

He felt Robbie's hands slide beneath his shirt, the smooth fingers caressing his skin. "I guess that makes two of us." Thank God the horse was only walking or he'd injure something important.

Emerging from the trees, Joey directed Twilight around the edge of the pasture, checking out the fence as the lumbering beasts munched on grass inside. They rode around the pasture, checking all the fencing before moving on. Riding fence was usually boring. But with Robbie along, it was wonderfully pleasant.

"Do you hear that?" Robbie asked in Joey's ear,

Joey shook his head no.

"Keep going. It seems to be getting louder."

"I hear it now. Sounds like an animal in trouble." He followed the sound until he saw what looked like a small furry body in the pasture. "Aw, looks like a cat got trampled."

The brush near them parted and Rex appeared carrying a kitten by the scruff of the neck. He took one look at them and loped back toward the barn, the kitten rocking in his grasp.

Robbie pointed, "There's crying over there."

"Stay here, I'll be right back." Sliding down, Joey handed Robbie the reins. "Just stay still, she won't move." Walking through the grass, he followed the sound until he came upon another kitten.

Picking up the black and white bundle of fur, he cradled the crying kitten in his hands and walked back to Robbie and Twilight. "Can you hold it?"

He handed the kitten to Robbie and very ungracefully remounted. Taking the kitten, he held it in one hand. "Hang on. I've got a little more fence to check, and we'll head back." He directed Twilight around the rest of the pasture since they were at the far edge anyway.

At the barn, they found Rex reclining in the shade near the barn door, a gray and white kitten climbing on the reclining dog. Joey handed Robbie the kitten and slid off again before setting the kitten on the ground. The little fur ball raced to its litter mate, both of them crawling all over the resting dog.

He heard footsteps on the gravel and saw Arie walking their way, his face as hard as granite. "Are you determined to get him hurt?" Joey was ready to fire back at him but turned and helped Robbie off Twilight instead. This wasn't his battle; it was Robbie's. "He shouldn't be on a horse, and definitely not alone. He can't see, for Christ's sake!"

As Arie began yelling, Joey looked at Robbie, wondering what the hell was going on. Arie stormed toward them. "What were you thinking? He could have fallen off and gotten hurt or worse!" Joey saw a change in Arie's expression, a new emotion joining the fear. His face softened slightly even if his voice didn't. "What's next, roping steers?" Joey stepped back and caught a glimpse of Robbie's face. The man was beautiful standing passively, letting Arie go on and on, but Joey could see the set of his mouth, his firm jaw.

"Are you done?" were the only words Robbie said, calmly and evenly. From the look on Robbie's face, Joey wasn't sure he'd want to be Arie right now. So he took Twilight's reins and steadied her as he waited for the fireworks.

Love Means ... NO Boundaries

ROBBIE didn't know what to think. He could still feel the horse beneath him and hear Arie's voice yelling at Joey. He felt Joey's hand brush his leg and place his foot in the stirrup. He took that as his cue to dismount, which he did with relative ease.

Up until now the day had been damn near perfect, helping in the kitchen and spending hours in the sun and air on horseback with Joey. Hell, he'd even gotten the courage to slide his hands beneath Joey's shirt. A few times he's slid his fingertips around his nipples and felt them pebble beneath his touch. Yes, Joey definitely made him horny. But now Arie had arrived and had jumped to all sorts of conclusions.

"Are you done?" He tried to keep his voice as level as he could, but he wanted to throttle Arie for yelling at Joey. He couldn't tell if Joey was angry because he hadn't said a thing. Finally, Arie started to wind down. "What in God's green earth has gotten into you?" That seemed to bring Arie's tirade to an end. "You're not my mother, for God's sake. You're my friend, or I thought you were." Robbie heard a sharp intake of breath.

"I am your friend." He sounded hurt.

"Then act like it."

"I am."

"No you're not. You're acting like an extension of my mother!" He hoped that would get Arie's attention. "I can't believe you called her and told her I got hurt, like some sort of spy." He heard what he thought was nervous shuffling. "You have to decide whose friend you are, mine or my mother's."

"I'm your friend. I've always been your friend." The plaintive tone told Robbie that Arie might be getting the idea.

"Then act like it. In the last few days I've done things I never thought I could. I realize that's because everyone's been sheltering me: you, my mama, my papa, everyone. Today I got to ride a horse. Tomorrow I'll be able to ride a tractor or take a ride on a motorcycle, whatever. The thing is, if you're my friend, you'll help me, not shelter me. Yes, I'm blind but that doesn't mean I should sit in a chair for the rest of my life because it's safe!"

Everything around him seemed to cease. The horse stopped her snorting. The kittens became quiet, even the wind seemed to hold its breath. Then he heard the clop of hooves and the crunch of feet behind him, growing softer.

"I'm sorry. I shouldn't have called your mom."

"No, you shouldn't have." Robbie wasn't ready to let him completely off the hook yet.

"And I shouldn't have yelled."

"That's true." Robbie folded his arms across his chest.

"Dang it, I was just worried about you."

Robbie felt the last of his anger and indignation fall away. "If I need help, I'll ask, but I need to do things for myself, and I need to see what I can do. And just for the record, I wasn't alone, I was with Joey." Silence. Robbie waited. He knew he had more patience than Arie.

"I'll try."

"Okay." Robbie smiled, and he felt Arie give him a hug.

"Is everything okay?" Joey asked as he approached, Robbie hearing his footsteps on the gravel.

"I think so." Robbie replied as Arie released his hug.

"Would you like to stay for lunch?" He felt Joey stand next to him, an arm snaking around his waist. Robbie smiled as Joey staked his claim. He could almost feel the testosterone in Joey's touch—it was a little more insistent than it usually was—but the electric attraction was instantly present.

"Are you sure? That would be very nice. Thank you."

Robbie heard a hint of surprise in his friend's voice, but let it go and allowed Joey to lead him toward the house. "What about the kittens?"

"They'll be fine. They're having a ball with Rex." Joey's voice felt so close, so intimate all of a sudden even though what he was saying was so ordinary.

Lunch was pleasant, though a little rushed, with people entering, eating, and then leaving again. At one point Robbie told Geoff he should consider a revolving door on the kitchen. Geoff had laughed along with the others at the table. Robbie gave up trying to keep all the hands voices straight and concentrated on those he already knew.

"Do you need anything?" Eli asked as he cleared the table.

"No, I don't think so."

"We'll be out for most of the afternoon, so call if you need anything." He felt the man's touch on his shoulder, and then the touch faded, and the back door opened and closed, leaving him alone with Joey and Arie.

"I've got work to do this afternoon." He heard Joey push back from the table.

Without thought, Robbie asked, "What are we doing?"

He could hear the pleasure in Joey's response. "I've got a field that's fallow, and I need to spread some organic fertilizer."

"Do you mean manure?" He heard the surprised revulsion in Arie's voice. "How can you stand the smell?"

Joey scoffed lightly, "You get used to it. When you have over a thousand head of cattle, you get a lot of manure."

"Will you use the tractor? Can I ride along with you?" Robbie asked excitedly.

"You want to spread manure?" The disbelief in Arie's voice was priceless.

"No, I want to ride in a tractor."

Arie began stuttering. "B-but…."

Robbie scowled at him to remind Arie of his earlier promise, and he wisely stopped talking.

"I have to get some things ready and check on the kittens. I'll come get you in half an hour." Joey touched his shoulder and then left the room, the screen door banging loudly.

"What's going on with you and him?" It came out slightly accusatory.

Robbie exhaled loudly. "I'm not sure. I like him, Arie, and I think he likes me."

"You mean likes you or *likes* you?" His voice did this weird swoopy thing.

"Arie, I know you're gay. You told me years ago."

"And you said you weren't."

He didn't know what to say to that. He was just beginning to understand his feelings. "I like him." A thought crossed him mind. "If you tell anyone, I'll rip your nuts off."

"Wh-what about your parents?" Robbie liked that Arie was getting nervous. It helped keep him in control.

"Look, Ma Bell, this concerns me and me alone." Arie could be such a gossip. "You say anything, and I'll never speak to you again."

Love Means … NO Boundaries

"You know they'll love you regardless of whether you're gay."

"Yeah, but…." Robbie swallowed. "Think about it." He tried to imagine Arie's expression but failed.

"Ohhh."

"Yeah, so keep your sweet little Dixie mouth shut."

He heard a heavy sigh. "I won't say anything, don't worry." Robbie felt Arie take him by the hand. "I promise." There was something strange in his voice, something Robbie couldn't place, but the back door opened and closed before he could ask.

"I'll be just a few minutes." Robbie heard Joey's footsteps through the house heading upstairs.

"You do know what he looks like don't you?" Arie whispered.

"He was in an accident. I know his face has scars, but they're not as bad as the ones on his spirit. He thinks he's ugly, and with the way other people treat him, it's no doubt why he feels that way. After all, I heard how you reacted."

"I know. I'm not proud of it, and I don't think he's ugly."

"He's really nice."

"I can see that." Footsteps approached, and their conversation tapered off as Joey entered the kitchen.

"I'm ready. Arie, do you want to go along?"

A chuckle followed. "Goodness no! I'll see you tomorrow at rehearsal. And Joey, it was nice to meet you." Arie said his goodbyes and left.

"How'd he get here anyway?" Robbie wondered out loud.

"He appears to have walked. I can see him heading toward the road." It got quiet and Robbie figured he was still watching. "He must be staying with the Rubas. They're the only ones close enough in that direction." Footsteps again. "Are you ready to go?"

Robbie got to his feet, putting on his sunglasses. "Ready, Freddy." He heard Joey laugh, and he wished he could always make him do that. He sounded so good when he laughed.

As they left the house, Robbie heard a low mechanical rumble getting closer, the ground vibrating. "Is that the tractor?"

"Yes." Joey spoke louder to be heard. "The guys have the spreader loaded and ready."

A sweet, nauseating smell filled his nose. "I'll say it's loaded." He fanned his hand in front of his nose. "Lead on. Let's spread some poop." He heard Joey laugh again and felt a hand on his arm, guiding him toward the source of the noise.

"You got it, Joey?" The man was almost yelling.

"Sure, Lumpy, no problem." The noise continued. "There are steps. Just be careful and I'll help you get in." Robbie felt Joey's touch, and then a hand placed his on the cool metal and a foot on the step. Slowly, he climbed up and inside, Joey guiding him until he was in the cab. "The seat's in front of you."

"How will you drive?"

"There's a passenger seat." He sat down and then felt Joey's breath on his lips just before he was softly kissed. "Are you comfortable?"

"Yeah, I didn't expect air conditioning." The cab door closed, shutting out most of the noise.

"Here we go." Joey sounded like an excited kid. Robbie felt the huge machine lurch forward, and then they were moving.

"This is so cool." He couldn't see, but he could feel the powerful machine as it transported them along the road.

"Did you and Arie have a good visit?"

Love Means ... NO Boundaries

"Yeah." He wasn't sure what to tell him about his discussion with Arie.

"He's in love with you, ya know"

"Arie? No way."

"He is, Robbie. I can see it in the way he looks at you."

"Do I detect a hint of jealousy?"

"Maybe."

Robbie wondered what it had taken Joey to admit that. "Arie's just a friend. I'm not interested in him that way." Robbie reached over and found Joey, leaning against him, letting their warmth mingle in the cool cabin.

Robbie felt the tractor turn, and the smooth ride of the road was replaced by bumps. He heard the engine change pitch and they slowed. "What's happening?"

"I engaged the spreader. It shouldn't take long."

Robbie felt one of Joey's arms slip around his waist as the tractor continued moving forward. Regardless of what was happening outside and what they were spreading, inside the cabin, everything was completely different. They rode quietly together. Occasionally, he'd feel a bump, but mostly he felt Joey holding him. It was wonderful being this close to him.

The motion stopped, and he heard gears changing. Then they began moving again and he felt them turn. The ride smoothed out and Robbie rested his head against Joey's shoulder.

They spent the afternoon traveling back and forth from the farm to the field. Robbie lost track of the number of times they made the trip. It didn't matter to him—he was alone with Joey and whenever he left the cabin and returned, Joey kissed him and settled in his seat, pulling them close together. Robbie couldn't help feeling that the others probably thought it strange that they were cuddling

77

inside a tractor, but he didn't care. It was wonderful because of who he was with. What they were doing didn't matter.

Robbie lost all tract of time and was surprised when he heard Joey turn off the engine. "What's happening? Are we done?"

"Yes. Eli should have dinner ready soon." Joey helped him out of the cab and to his surprise, pulled him close and kissed him hard. "You've been warming me up all afternoon." Robbie put his arms around Joey and held on for the incredible ride. Joey's lips felt and tasted so good, his tongue playing and gently probing as they kissed.

"Are you two coming in for dinner?" He heard Geoff's voice behind them, but Joey didn't stop. He just pulled him tighter. He heard Geoff say something about having dessert first as Joey pulled away.

"Joey." Robbie felt embarrassed that they'd been seen kissing.

A work-roughened hand slid gently along his cheek. "There's nothing to be embarrassed about. Geoff always told me that this was a safe place and had been for a long time. His dad was gay. He died a few years ago. Len, he was Geoff's dad's partner, he'll be back in a few days with Chris. They've been together almost five years now. So you see there's nothing to worry about." He felt Joey guiding him forward.

"What about the other guys?"

"Pete's married to Geoff's cousin and Lumpy's cool. All the other guys know. Geoff wouldn't hire them if they weren't supportive. Like I said, this is a safe place."

Robbie felt Joey hug him close, and he whispered, "Can we eat quickly?"

"Whatever you want, cutie."

Dinner was wonderful. Afterward they gathered in the living room with the television on. It'd been a long day, and they were all tired. Robbie heard Joey talking with the guys about crops and such, so he made his way carefully to his room and found his violin on the dresser where he'd left it. Opening the case, he retrieved his instrument and bow, drawing it over the strings. The music filled the small room as he let himself go, let his mind play over all the wonderful things he'd done that day. His fingers zoomed over the strings as the bow became an extension of his emotions. The joy and thrill of riding with Joey, the fun they'd had kissing in the tractor, finding the wee kittens, all raced through his body and screamed for release, which is exactly what he did. Robbie filled the room with the wonder and ecstasy of doing fantastic new things.

Robbie completely lost track of time, and as he drew out the final note, he heard soft applause. "That was beautiful. What were you playing?"

"Nothing in particular." Robbie set his instrument in the case.

"No," he heard Joey take a step into the room. "I meant what were you feeling as you played?"

Robbie felt himself smile. "All the things we did today." He expected some sort of answer. Instead, he felt hands slide down his shoulders and lips press to his in a searing kiss. Robbie kissed back and held on, trusting Joey would guide them to a soft landing. The kisses continued as his cheeks and face were caressed, fingers wound through his hair as he felt himself being guided. "Where are we going?" Robbie figured Joey would lead him to the bed, and unless he was all turned around, which was possible, the bed was in the other direction.

"To my bed." Joey didn't step back or move away. Somehow, he guided them, entwined together across the hall. When he heard the door close, he felt Joey slip his hands beneath his shirt and lift. Robbie raised his arms, and the shirt slipped off. Hands caressed his skin, wandering hands that kept moving. "You feel so good, look so good."

Robbie felt the lips move away from his and attach themselves to a nipple, sucking and swirling. Robbie thought his head was going to explode. Then they moved, swirling around the other one. "Joey." It felt so good. He could hardly believe this was happening to him. He could feel it, but it was so incredible that he almost thought it was happening to someone else. The kisses traveled lower, and he felt a tongue slide across his abdomen, lips placing wet kisses on his skin. He felt a hand at his belt, opening it, and his pants slid lower before sliding over his hips and down his legs.

"You're so beautiful, Robbie. You skin is like honey silk, smooth and perfect." A hand glided down his chest and over his stomach before circling around his cock. As soon as Joey touched him he gasped in surprise. No one had ever touched him that way before and damn if it didn't feel a million times better than when he did it himself. Stepping out of his pants, he felt himself being lowered onto the bed, and he heard Joey's shoes thunk on the floor followed by the chink of a belt as it, too, met the floor. Then the bed bounced, and he felt Joey's warm breath against his lips. "I know you've never done this before, so if I do something you don't like, you have to tell me."

"Okay, I promise." He felt those lips travel down his body again, the hand wrapped around him. And then he was engulfed in hot wetness. "What's happening?" He could barely breathe as he felt what could only be Joey's lips sliding down his length. Robbie found himself breathing like he'd run a marathon as Joey took him deep while fingers slid over his balls.

He had no idea how long he could hold out, the pressure already building. He wanted this to last. It just felt so indescribably good. "Joey!" Then he felt the wetness slip away.

"Are you okay?"

"Uh huh, it just feels so good," Robbie panted, as he tried to lift his head off the pillow.

Love Means ... NO Boundaries

"Good. That's how it's supposed to feel." Then it was back, the hot wetness taking him deep, sucking hard, and he gave himself over to it and let himself feel all the pleasure that Joey was so freely giving him. The thought that Joey was doing this for him, making him feel this way, filled him to overflowing, and he cried out, not holding back as he came in a wave of pleasure.

When he regained his breath, he sat up and felt Joey's lips against his. This time he pulled Joey close and let his own hands explore. "Can I?" He didn't really know what he wanted to ask, he just knew that he wanted to try everything Joey had showed him and more.

"Whatever you like."

He felt Joey turn on the bed, lying down with him on top. He liked that. He didn't get a lot of chances to feel like he was in charge of anything. Using his hands as guides, he found Joey's nipples and kissed them, the buds hardening beneath his touch. As he tasted, he heard Joey moan softly and felt him thrust his chest forward. Taking that as a good sign, he increased the pressure, and the moans got louder. "Joey, can I taste you, like you did me?"

"You can, but you don't have to." He heard Joey's breathy voice between soft pants. He wanted to give Joey the same pleasure Joey had given him, but he wasn't sure how to do it, and he felt a little too embarrassed to ask for help. Using his hands as guides again, he slid down Joey's body and felt his way to Joey's erection.

It was long and thick and felt good in his hand. Thinking about what he liked, he stroked the length, getting to know how it felt. "Robbie!!" He smiled as Joey began writhing beneath him. He leaned forward and slid his tongue tentatively over the length, and his mouth exploded with the intense taste of Joey. He'd licked his skin and kissed him, but this was intense.

Opening his mouth, he slid his lips over the head and down the shaft before pulling back. "Take it easy." Robbie tried again, and this time it felt better, in fact it felt amazing. The feel of Joey sliding across his tongue, the sounds he was making along with the little movements of his hips. He tried to remember what Joey had done that he liked so much and did his best to imitate. He heard soft moans and cries and figured he was doing okay. "Robbie, I'm close." He tried harder and heard Joey cry out as his mouth filled with Joey's release. He did his best to swallow and then climbed back up Joey's body and felt himself being cuddled. Joey's hands held him close, and he felt lips softly kissing his face.

As they lay together, Joey's hands sliding over his skin, Robbie wondered what he was going to do. Joey was so kind, thoughtful, and caring, and Robbie wondered how he was ever going to be able to leave and go home at the end of next week. He was falling for Joey. He knew that. But he wasn't sure if it was some sort of infatuation or if he was falling in love.

"What are you thinking about?" Joey whispered against his lips.

"I'm thinking about next week." He couldn't keep the worry out of his voice, even though he tried.

"I know, Robbie. Me too." He felt Joey's arms tighten around him and he got the feeling that Joey was holding him as a shield to ward off the same impending worries that he was feeling.

Love Means ... NO Boundaries

CHAPTER 5

THE cloudy coolness was great for weeding the garden, and Joey found himself on his hands and knees weaving through the rows, plucking errant plants that had the nerve to invade his vegetables. Robbie sat on the grass nearby with Rex resting next to him and two kittens climbing over the dog and Robbie's lap as they played.

The last few days had been some of the best Joey could remember since his accident. He and Robbie went riding every day, checking fences, and inspecting fields. When Robbie was at rehearsal, Joey would redouble his efforts, getting all the unpleasant jobs done so he could spend as much time with Robbie as possible. But the nights, those were his favorite. He and Robbie got to be alone, equals in the dark, exploring each other's bodies.

"Is it going to rain?" Robbie called, and Joey looked up just in time to see a kitten trying to climb Robbie's chest.

"I hope so. They've been promising for a few days and the fields could use it." Joey went back to his weeding. "I just hope we get a good steady rain instead of a deluge." He heard Robbie's laughter and saw the kitten cuddled against Robbie's neck, licking his face with her rough tongue. "Have you thought about names for them?"

"Me?" Robbie laughed again.

"Sure, Rex seems to have adopted you, and they're his kittens, so you name them."

More laughter rang out, and Joey smiled to himself, pulling his eyes away from Robbie and returning to work. Both of them became quiet.

Joey heard movement from where Robbie was sitting, and then the warm tones of the violin floated over the yard. Without thinking Joey stopped working and listened, watching Robbie as he played.

The tune was unfamiliar, but captivating. Even the kittens stopped running, curling up next to Rex, resting their heads as Robbie played. The music felt happy, joyful, and Joey knew that Robbie was playing exactly what they were both feeling. Joey listened, the weeding forgotten as the musical serenade reflected his own happiness.

Pulling his attention back to his task, he listened and smiled, pulling the weeds to the rhythm of Robbie's music.

As the last note died away, Joey heard someone clear his throat. "I didn't want to interrupt."

Joey looked up and grinned, slipped off his gloves, and stood up, hugging the man standing on the edge of the garden. "Len. When did you get home?" The older man returned his hug.

"Last night," Len said as Joey stepped back. "Who's this?"

Joey remembered his manners. "This is Robbie. He's in town with the youth symphony. He's staying with us for the next week."

Robbie put his violin in the case and stood up. Joey watched as Len stepped forward. Robbie held out his hand and waited. Len looked a little confused before walking over and shaking Robbie's hand. "It's a pleasure to meet you."

"Same here. Joey's told me a lot about you." Robbie bent down and felt around, putting his instrument back in the case as they felt the first drops of rain.

Joey reached down and picked up a kitten. "Can you make it back to the house?"

"Yes." Robbie picked up his case and began retracing his steps back to the house.

"He's blind?" Joey heard Len mutter almost under his breath.

"Yeah." Joey picked up his gloves and tools before heading back to the house. "He's absolutely amazing." He carried his things to the house, watching Robbie to make sure he was okay and setting his tools in the mudroom before going inside.

A small crowd had gathered around the kitchen table including Chris, Len's partner for the last five years. The kitchen was full of voices, and Joey gently guarded Robbie to an empty chair.

"Chris, this is Robbie," Joey said and greetings followed as the conversation continued to swirl among everyone, including Pete, Lumpy, and the other hands. They anxiously awaited details of Chris and Len's cruise. Chris could really tell a story and had everyone laughing with tales of their experiences aboard ship—from the man who hooked the tablecloth in his pants at dinner, taking it and the dishes along with him as he exited the dining room, to the kid who lost his bathing suit on the water slide.

"Is the chainsaw still in the tool shed?" Len asked Geoff as he put his coffee cup in the sink. "There must have been a storm while we were gone because we've got a few limbs down at our place." Len had moved in with Chris a few years earlier, and they appeared extremely happy.

"It's on the tool bench."

The guys took that as a sign that the stories were over for now and got up to leave, saying goodbye before heading home.

"I'll get it and put it in the trunk," Chris volunteered as he got up, his hand traveling lovingly over Len's shoulders.

"So, Robbie," Len started. "How'd you get messed up with this group?"

Joey explained about Mari being desperate, and Robbie told him about all the things he'd done on the farm. Regardless of being blind, Robbie's eyes shone as he told Len about Joey helping him ride a horse.

"I take it you're having a good time."

"The best!" Robbie squeezed Joey's thigh under the table, and Joey did his best not to squeal in surprise.

The back door banged, and Chris walked back in the kitchen. "All set." He took a seat around the table.

"Geoff, that's a terrific motorcycle in there, is it yours? It looks really cool."

Most eyes around the table turned to Joey. "It's mine," he said as he tried to figure out how to disappear into the floor.

"Shit, I'm sorry. It looked cool, and I guess I forgot."

It was funny, but the last few days, Joey had forgotten. The accident and his face didn't matter so much when he was around Robbie.

"What are you going to do with it?" Chris asked.

Joey shrugged, but it was Robbie that spoke up. "Take me for a ride." It wasn't a question.

"I don't think I can." Joey wasn't sure he'd ever be able to ride that bike again, or any motorcycle for that matter. When he got the courage to look at Robbie, he saw that beautiful face set in a completely foreign expression, but he said nothing. Joey had the sneakiest suspicion he hadn't heard the last of it.

Eli got up from the table. "I've got horses to tend, rain or not." He leaned forward and kissed Geoff. "I'll be in later, and it's your turn to cook." Eli smiled knowingly.

"Dinner in town, it is." Everyone laughed, including Eli, and after getting another kiss from his lover, Eli headed to the barn. Chris said he needed to make a few calls and went into the other room.

"I should get things done too." Geoff put his dishes away and headed into the office.

"I should rehearse before tomorrow's performance." Joey handed Robbie his violin case, and he went upstairs, leaving Len and Joey alone.

Len didn't waste any time. "So are you and Robbie an item?"

"For now." Joey tried not to think about the end of the week and Robbie going home.

"I thought so. You're smiling more and you seem... happy. Something I haven't seen in a while."

"I am happy and scared at the same time. He goes back to Mississippi in a week." He tried to keep the disappointment at bay.

"How do you feel about him?"

Joey looked into Len's face and saw only care. Len was as close to a father as Joey'd ever had, and he almost worshipped the man.

"I think...." Joey couldn't say it. He wasn't ready to admit out loud how he felt. If he did he'd have to deal with it.

Joey felt a hand on his arm. "There's truth to the old saying that it's better to have loved and lost than never to have loved at all. Our hearts decide who we get to love, but only God decides how long we have them to love. You have to make the most of the time you have, be it seven days, seven months, or seven years."

"I don't know how I can let him go." Joey wiped his eyes. "He's one of the most wonderful people I've ever known. He made spreading manure and riding fence fun." Everyone hated those jobs.

"You won't have a choice. All you can do is enjoy the time you have."

The sound of Robbie's violin drifted through the house. "Thanks, Len."

"What are you going to do?" Joey saw the knowing look.

"I suppose if Robbie can be brave enough to ride a horse, I can try getting back on one." Both men stood, and before Joey could leave, Len pulled him into a hug. "I'm glad you're home, Len." A glint of gold caught Joey's eye. "Is that new?"

Len pulled up his sleeve to expose the large watch. "Yeah, Chris bought it for me while we were gone." The huge gold watch shone in the light.

"Is it real?" God, it must have cost a fortune.

"Yeah. Chris insisted on buying it for me when I looked in a jeweler's window in St. Maarten." Len didn't seem too thrilled.

"It's nice. But I guess I never thought of you wearing something like that."

"Me either." Len wasn't ostentatious in the least, but since Chris's business had taken off, he'd been buying Len expensive things. Len had met him when they'd hired Chris to help on the farm. He was trying to earn extra money to get his business off the ground at the time.

Love Means ... NO Boundaries

"Oh." Joey figured Chris had bought the watch as a gift, and Len was too nice to say it wasn't his style. Joey looked toward the living room. "Is something wrong?"

Len looked for a second like he was debating in his mind. "No. It's just that Chris has been so busy lately, and it's almost like he buys me things to make up for him not being around."

Joey smiled conspiratorially. "You always told me when I was young that you either spend time or spend money."

"That's right, but I wish Chris would spend a little more time. Not that I'm faulting him or don't think he loves me, but...." Len stopped himself. "You don't need to hear this. Go on and spend time with that sweet young man."

Joey wanted to help but wasn't sure what to do. Seeing Len unhappy, even slightly, wasn't something he liked.

"Go on. I'll be fine." Len walked toward where Chris was on the phone and Joey saw Chris open his arms and hug Len to him as he completed his call.

The music continued, drawing him like a siren's song up the stairs. He found Robbie sitting on the edge of his bed with a four-legged audience already in place. Joey sat next to Rex and scratched the dog's ears. "Please don't stop playing."

Robbie lifted his bow again and continued his playing as Joey descended into his own thoughts. Len was right about enjoying the time they had. At the end of the week, Robbie would go home to his family's house with housekeepers and things Joey could only dream about. But as long as he was here, Joey was going to make the most of their time together. Joey knew he could never fit in Robbie's world. If money could cause problems in Len's relationship with Chris, what would it be like when Robbie returned home to every convenience and lack of worry that money could provide? No. Whatever hopes he may have allowed himself to have would have to go. They had their week. That was it, and he intended to accept it. But, God, he didn't want to.

JOEY was so deep in his own thoughts that he didn't realize Robbie had stopped playing until he started again. This time a slow somber melody, echoing his mood, filled the room as the rain beat on the windows. Listening to that song, he hoped it was something Robbie had to play as opposed to how he was feeling as well. The last thing he wanted was to make Robbie melancholy too. As the music came to a soft end, Robbie set down his instrument. "What's on your mind? And don't say nothing, I can tell something's bothering you."

"I'm just thinking, that's all." Joey leaned across the bed, touching Robbie's cheek before kissing him softly.

As soon as their lips touched, the room lightened and filtered rays of sunshine shone through the window as if Mother Nature herself were trying to dispel Joey's gloom. "How much longer do you need to rehearse?"

"About an hour. Why?"

Joey stood up. "I'll leave you to it. I've got some things to do." With another kiss, Joey got up from the bed, and after another kiss, he left the room before turning back and watching as Robbie picked up his instrument.

"You don't have to stand there." Robbie smiled as he placed the violin under his chin.

"I like to watch you." Joey saw a look of concentration on Robbie's face as he drew the bow across the strings, eliciting the first beautiful note. Joey sighed softly and headed downstairs and outside, walking to the equipment shed.

His bike was exactly where he'd left it, the tarp disheveled but still covering the motorcycle. The machine had once been his pride and joy, but now he could barely bring himself to pull the tarp off. "Grow a pair, will ya!" Pulling off the tarp, he set it on the floor and looked at the purple and white cycle. Forcing himself forward, he ran his hands over the now-repaired bike. Only a few scratches indicated what happened those months ago.

While he'd been recuperating, Geoff had arranged for the repairs, but Joey had barely looked at it.

Len's words the first time he'd been thrown from a horse popped into his head. "You can't be ruled by fear and what-ifs." Len had made him get right back in the saddle.

Kicking back the stand, he walked the bike outside. The clouds had parted and everything felt new and clean, the sun sending bright rays that shone and glistened in the damp air.

Methodically, he inspected the motorcycle, checking the fluids and filling the gas tank. He kept telling himself that he had to do this. Len would have told him he'd waited too long already.

Taking a deep breath and slipping on his helmet before throwing his leg over and resting his butt on the seat, Joey steadied the bike between his legs as he kicked back the stand. Turning the key, he heard the starter turn over, but the engine didn't catch. Trying again, he pumped the throttle and turned the key again, and the engine roared to life.

He almost shut it off and walked away, but instead he sat on the rest and eased out the clutch and he was moving down the drive and onto the street.

Opening it up, he glided down the empty road, the air buffeting his body. The nervousness was still there, but so was something else: the freedom and exhilaration he'd felt whenever he rode. But now it was tempered with caution. "I can do this." Turning the corner, he rode toward town before turning again and completing a country circuit back to the farm.

When he pulled in, he saw Len standing in the farmyard with Robbie standing next to him, huge grins on their faces. As he pulled up, Chris came out of the house, joining Len before both men waved and got in their car, heading home. Robbie was grinning at him, practically bouncing from foot to foot.

Joey slipped off his helmet. "Would you really like a ride?" He turned off the engine.

"I really would."

He wasn't sure how he felt about it. What if something happened? He could never forgive himself if Robbie got hurt. "I'm not sure it's a good idea." Joey's stomach started doing flip-flops at the thought. But it was seeing that look of expectant excitement on Robbie's face fade that made him relent.

"All right, a short ride. Let me get the other helmet." Joey put down the stand, got off the bike, and went into the equipment shed, returning with a white helmet. "I'll help you with it, but you need to take off your glasses." Gently he slipped the helmet on Robbie's head, fastening the chin strap and lowering the sun visor before helping Robbie onto the back of the motorcycle seat. "Once I get on, put your feet here." He placed Robbie's foot on the holders. "And hold on to me just like you do when we ride Twilight."

"Okay."

Robbie got on the cycle and felt Robbie grip his hips. Checking to make sure Robbie's feet were in the right place, he started the engine and kicked back the stand before slowly moving the bike forward.

There was nothing coming, so Joey turned onto the street and accelerated, feeling Robbie grip him tighter. He didn't go very fast, and he could hear Robbie say something. Not sure, Joey pulled off the road. "Are you okay?"

The helmet nodded vigorously. "This is incredible."

Love Means ... NO Boundaries

"Okay, hang on." Joey pulled back onto the road and opened her up, keeping a careful eye on the road and their speed. He wasn't taking any chances. He had precious cargo behind him, after all. It felt good to have the familiar feeling of power beneath him, and he loved the feeling of Robbie behind him.

Turning north, he headed along the country road, driving over rolling hills, keeping an eye on everything. Once he relaxed a little, he started enjoying the ride. Then he felt a new sensation pressing against his backside. Robbie was hard, his erection pressing insistently against Joey's butt. Damn, his Robbie was a daredevil. His Robbie… he pushed the thought away and concentrated on the road.

Joey wanted to ask how Robbie was doing, but the hardness against him told him pretty much what he needed to know. He turned the bike again and remained at a slow speed. There was a blind curve up ahead, and he took it with care and increased speed, throttling up just as a car pulled out of a driveway ahead of him. Joey slowed but the car wasn't picking up speed, and he felt a tingling and tightening throughout his entire being. It was like his body remembered and reacted. Suddenly the brake lights came on, and the car pulled to a stop in his lane and Joey put on the brakes, tires screeching beneath him. "Jesus Christ, not again!" Joey yelled into his helmet as another car came toward them in the other lane cutting off his escape route.

The pain and fear from the last accident came flooding back along with another worry about Robbie sitting behind him.

ROBBIE felt the seat swerve and jump beneath him, and he couldn't figure out what was going on. Then the bike pitched him forward into Joey before bouncing him up off the seat. He heard the sound of gravel beneath the wheels, and they were sliding again, first to one side and then the other. He had no idea what to do and felt completely helpless. "Joey!" he called out into the helmet that surrounded his head, but it hardly mattered. Gripping Joey as hard as he could, he held on to him as the bike kept moving but eventually slowed down.

"Oh my God! Are you okay?" He heard a female voice call out as he felt them stop and the bike engine died. All he could hear was his own breath reverberating in his ears in the helmet. "You're not hurt are you?" The female voice got louder, but Joey hardly paid attention, he just sat there on the back of the bike, gripping Joey for dear life, his heart still racing a million miles a minute.

"I think we're okay." He heard Joey's muffled voice answer as they both stayed stark still. He felt Joey turn around. "Are you all right?" Joey's voice was clearer, and he nodded his head, not trusting his voice enough to answer directly. He didn't seem to be hurt, just scared.

"Dad!" The female voice called out. "What were you doing?" The voice got farther away. "You're not supposed to be driving." There must have been an answer because he heard the voice again. "To get the mail? You almost caused an accident." He felt Joey's hand on his arm.

"I think we'll get home."

Robbie nodded again, refusing to let go of Joey as the engine started again, and they began to move. They felt like they were turning, bouncing slightly. Then the ride became smooth and they rode slowly back to the farm.

Robbie felt himself tense at every bump or turn. Then he heard gravel beneath the wheels, and Joey turned off the engine, but neither of them moved. "We need to get off." Slowly, Robbie released his grip and straightened himself up before pulling his feet on the ground and getting off the bike. He heard Joey's feet on the gravel before feeling his fingers on the chin strap, and the helmet lifted off his head, and he could hear normally again. "Are you okay?" He heard Joey whisper softly.

"Yeah, I'm fine. What happened?" Robbie tried to keep some of the emotion out of his voice, but he didn't think he succeeded.

"I almost hit a car that stopped in the road. Some old guy turned in front of us. I drove across a driveway and onto a lawn to keep us from hitting him." Joey's voice sounded cold and distant. He heard footsteps again and the soft whir of gears. He figured Joey was putting the bike away.

Robbie waited for Joey to return, but he didn't. Instead Robbie found himself standing where Joey had gotten off the bike, wondering where the hell he was. "Joey?" Nothing at all, just the sound of the farm around him.

"Robbie." He heard Geoff's voice calling from what he hoped was the farmhouse and footsteps running toward him. "What happened?"

"I don't really know." He was so confused and hurt. Joey had forgotten him. "Something happened while we were riding, and he brought me back here."

"Where's Joey?" He could hear definite annoyance in Geoff's voice.

"I don't know." He thought he was going to cry, but swallowed hard instead. "I thought he was putting the bike away, but he never came back." Robbie didn't know what to make of it, and then he felt Geoff's hand on his arm, leading him across the yard.

"We're almost at the back door." Robbie felt the step with his toe and climbed into the house with Geoff gently guiding him inside and to the kitchen table."

"How was the ride?" Eli's bright voice cut through his own gloom.

"It was great until someone pulled out in front of us. Joey managed to avoid it and saved us. It was a rough ride, but we were both okay. When we got back here, he helped me off the bike, and took off." Robbie settled in a chair.

"Joey left him standing in the yard," Geoff supplied, annoyance in his voice.

More conversation went on around him, but he didn't pay attention. He knew both of them were upset by Joey's behavior, but he needed to think, and there was one place he could always think. Getting up from the table, he made his way through the house and upstairs. In the bedroom, he found his violin case sitting where he'd left it and slowly opened the case, taking out the instrument.

Instead of putting it to his chin, he ran his fingers over the smooth wood, the warmth and familiarity of the musical artist's craft comforting the internal ache. Picking up his bow, he settled on the edge of the bed and positioned the instrument, drawing the bow over the strings. The notes came forth from deep inside his mind, the confusion and helplessness all coming out through the violin. Brahms' German Requiem flowed through his mind. He could hear the entire piece: the orchestra, the choir, all accompanying him as he played. Tears ran down his face as he continued playing, expressing his own loss. As a child he often thought he'd been lucky he'd had a chance to see before his defective genes had taken away his sight, but in truth it made it harder, just like now. He'd been given the gift of freedom and encouragement, and in one moment he'd been left standing helplessly in the yard by someone he thought cared about him.

He played for hours, completely losing himself in the music. A soft knock on the door brought him back to himself, and he put down the instrument, pressing the button on his watch. The mechanical voice told him it was nine-thirty as he heard the door open. "I brought you something to eat." Eli's said softly. "You didn't come down for dinner, and none of us wanted to disturb you."

Robbie set down the violin, and he felt a plate being set on his lap and a glass pressed into his hand. "It's just a sandwich. I can bring you something else if you'd like."

"Thank you." Robbie was so thirsty; he drank most of the milk in a single gulp before setting the glass on the nightstand. Then he felt around the plate before picking up the sandwich. "Is Joey back?" He wanted to know and didn't want to know at the same time.

"He came in a few hours ago and went right back outside without saying a single word to anyone." Eli sounded concerned. "I wish I knew what was wrong."

Robbie finished the sandwich and milk, and Eli took the dishes. "Do you want to come downstairs with me?" Robbie shook his head. He didn't want to go anywhere. "Are you still hungry?"

"No, thank you." Robbie picked up his violin again and began playing. He didn't even hear the door close. He had no idea how long he played, but when he stopped the house was completely quiet, and he was completely drained. Putting his violin away, he wiped his face and found that his cheeks were wet. Getting up, he set the case on the dresser and opened the door. He heard scampering, and then the bed creaked. Smiling, he got ready for bed and crawled beneath the covers, Rex curling up next to him.

Robbie couldn't sleep. Instead, he lay in the bed listening to the dog snore, and occasionally he'd feel him running in his sleep, legs going as fast as they could. Robbie kept hoping that he'd hear his door open, and he'd hear Joey's voice; hoping that Joey would join him in bed and take him into his arms; and hoping he'd explain what had happened. Instead he got nothing but loneliness. Robbie tried to sleep, but it wouldn't come.

Robbie pushed the button on his watch, the voice telling him it was just after two in the morning. Huffing to himself he heard Rex snuffle as he got out of bed. Feeling his way, he found the door and opened it silently. Taking the now familiar three steps across the hall, he found Joey's closed door and put his hand on the knob and stopped, getting up his courage. He turned the knob and pushed open the door. He heard nothing, no soft breathing, nothing… at first.

"Robbie?"

The single word was enough for him to be able to follow. Walking in the room, he closed the door and walked up to the bed. "What did you think you were doing today?" He swung his hand and was rewarded by the smack of skin on skin. "You left me stranded in the middle of the yard. I didn't know where I was or how to get anywhere." He got louder as his anger took over. "I trusted you, and you abandoned me!" He swung again and felt a hand catch his wrist. "How could you do that?" Robbie's emotions were getting the best of him now, and he tried to pull his arm away so he could go back to his room.

"I-I'm sorry." The despair in Joey's voice made him stop struggling and listen. "The thought of hurting you is…." He heard Joey's voice begin to break, and he felt the hand let go of his wrist.

Part of him wanted to just leave and hurt Joey as much as he'd been hurt, but another part, a bigger part, was about what Joey had to say. Making his decision, he sat on the edge of the bed. "I'm listening." He folded his arms over his chest.

"I'm sorry I did that to you." Robbie heard a sniffle and knew Joey was crying and probably had been crying. "I almost got you killed when we were riding, and I thought you'd never want to see me again, not that I could blame you."

"What happened? Was it like before?" He felt a lump forming in his own throat.

"Yeah. Someone pulled out in front of us, and then he stopped. Turned out it was a really old man going out to pick up his mail. He obviously didn't see us and turned into the road. But then he stopped."

"How is that your fault?" Robbie waited for Joey to answer.

"I should have been prepared, gone slower."

God, he could hear the pain in Joey's voice, and it made his own eyes water.

"I couldn't stop in time and turned into the driveway and ended up stopping on the lawn."

Robbie let out his held breath. "Is that what this is about?" He swatted the blanket near him. "You saved us. Did we get in an accident? No. Did we hit anything? No. All we got was a bumpy ride for a few seconds, and you stopped us safely."

"But I almost killed you." The near grief in his voice was plainly evident.

"But you didn't. Instead your quick thinking got us stopped safely." Robbie took a big breath. "You did nothing wrong at all... until we got back to the farm. You let your fear take over, and you left me. I trusted you, and you left me."

Robbie heard Joey sniffle. "I thought you'd hate me for almost getting you injured or worse. Jesus, instead I hurt you by leaving you alone." Robbie felt Joey touch his arm. "I'm sorry. That's the last thing I wanted."

For the first time in hours, Robbie felt his stomach start to unwind. "I spent the last few hours thinking I'd done something wrong." His anger and frustration started to ramp up again. "I thought you were mad at me because I pressured you into taking for the ride in the first place."

Robbie waited and heard Joey laugh softly. "We're a pair aren't we?"

"I guess we are."

Robbie was about to get up when he felt Joey's arms around him, pulling him against the warmth of his body. Hands moved soothingly along his back as he was hugged tightly, like he was something precious.

"Don't ever abandon me again," Robbie chastised softly just before his lips were taken and hands guided him under the covers. This was what Robbie had been hoping for earlier in the evening, that Joey would make love to him. Up until now Robbie had let Joey lead them in their nighttime endeavors. He smiled as he recalled his nanna's term for sex. But this time he returned Joey's kisses with gusto, using his weight to push Joey back against the bedding. He felt Joey trying to take charge, but Robbie wasn't giving up that easily and continued kissing him into the mattress until he felt Joey capitulate beneath him.

Robbie reveled in the control. He had so little of it in his life.

"Take what you want, Robbie." The words were an invitation he'd never received. He spent so much of his life under the control and guidance of others. Robbie felt his heart expand with forgiveness and wonder at the trust Joey was showing in him.

Robbie felt Joey's hands slide down his back and under the elastic of his briefs, cupping his butt.

"Lift your hips."

Complying, he felt the fabric slide over his hips and down his legs. Working them off, Robbie sighed softly as he felt Joey against him, skin to skin. Robbie kept kissing, his hands exploring the acres of hot skin beneath him, his hands forming a clear picture of every contour of Joey's body. "You always say I'm beautiful, but so are you."

Love Means ... NO Boundaries

"No I'm not." Robbie could hear the disbelief in Joey's voice.

"Yes you are." Robbie slid his hand down Joey's hip and across his belly. "I like this spot, right here." Joey laughed slightly as Robbie tickled him before capturing his tasty lips again. "Besides, it's not how you look on the outside that counts. It's what's on the inside that matters."

Robbie began kissing again in earnest, slowly rocking back and forth, his cock sliding on Joey's skin. *Don't abandon me.* He kept kissing as their erections continued rubbing together, sliding along hips and stomach. *I'm not helpless.* The intensity increased as Robbie feasted on Joey with his mouth, hands, and body, excitement building as they rocketed toward release. *I can do anything.* The surge of adrenaline with this last realization brought Robbie to climax, a silent cry swallowed within Joey's own.

Robbie let himself go and felt Joey catch him, drawing him close, lips kissing gently, adoringly as they both struggled to catch their breath.

"Don't do it again," Robbie chastised softly.

He felt Robbie smile against his lips. "I won't." He was encircled by strong arms and drawn against warm skin. A cloth cleaned him, and the warmth returned as the sheet was drawn over them. "I promise."

Robbie heard the soft, meaningful tone in Joey's voice, leaving so much unsaid. He knew what Joey was thinking, because he was thinking the exact same thing. He wanted to say it— they were just three little words—but he didn't. He was going home in less than a week, and everything would change. He heard Joey mutter his "I promise" again, and this time Robbie answered, "Me too."

The bed shook as Rex jumped up, curling near Robbie's feet. He waited a few seconds and heard soft mews followed by scampering signaling that the kittens had joined them in bed as well. "Have you thought about names for them? There's a boy and a girl."

"How about Mimi and Marcello. I just love *La Bohème*."

Joey laughed richly. "Mimi and Marcello, it is." Settling them on the bed, Joey held him close, and it wasn't long until the dog's soft breathing was joined by their own.

CHAPTER 6

JOEY woke with Robbie in his arms. Today was their last day together. Tomorrow morning he'd have to take Robbie back to the school so he could catch the bus that would take him away. He tried not to let himself get upset. He'd promised himself that he'd make the most of the time they had together, and they had. Together they'd ridden Twilight all around the farm, and they'd ridden the tractor together. Joey had even let Robbie drive the tractor. Well, he'd had Robbie sit on his lap and together they'd driven the tractor. With each new experience came a round of hot explorative sex once they went to bed. The man was truly a daredevil.

"What are you thinking about?" He heard Robbie's sleepy voice.

Joey sighed. "The fact that you go home tomorrow." He really didn't want to think about it too hard. This was their last day together, and he wanted to enjoy every minute of it. "I thought we could go riding this morning and swimming this afternoon."

Robbie's phone interrupted him, and he cringed as Robbie answered his mother's call. Over the last two weeks, he'd become accustomed to what he referred to as Robbie's pants alarm. That woman always seemed to call at the most inconvenient moments. Crossing his hands behind his head, he waited for Robbie to finish the call and then found himself surrounded by the body of the cutest man he'd ever met in his life. "You were saying?" Joey inquired as a finger swirled around a nipple, head resting on his shoulder.

"I was going to ask if you had rehearsal this morning."

"Nope." Robbie's tongue slid along his skin. "I'm all yours until the performance this evening." They heard noise in the hall as Geoff and Eli went downstairs. "But I think it's time to get up." Robbie lifted the covers, but Joey caught him and pulled him into a kiss.

"Okay, now you can get up." Joey watched as Robbie got out of bed, that tight little butt swaying as Robbie made his way along the bed and toward the door. Robbie had just reached the door when Joey jumped from the bed and caught Robbie around the waist. He let out a yelp and began giggling as Joey carried him back to bed.

"Joey," he said as he laughed joyfully while Joey carried him back to the bed. "You need to get to work."

"No I don't, I have the day off. Eli said I should spend the whole day with you." He set Robbie back on the bed and began kissing him, and soon their kissing progressed to other wonderful things.

They finally came down the stairs after everyone else was outside. "I thought we'd go swimming, and I was wondering if you'd like to ask if Arie wanted to come." Over the last week, he and Arie had started to become friends. Joey found that he and Arie had more in common than they thought, not the least of which was that they both cared for Robbie.

"You mean it? I think he's been a little lonely."

"Of course. Tell him we'll leave in an hour or so." Joey began making them some breakfast while Robbie made the call.

Love Means ... NO Boundaries

"He's on his way over." Robbie closed the phone and Joey looked over, seeing the smile on that sweet face. "Thank you."

"You're welcome." He'd do anything today to keep that look on Robbie's face.

Joey finished making breakfast and brought their plates to the table, telling Robbie what was where on his plate as the back door opened and banged closed. "Hey, Arie. Have you had breakfast?"

"Yes, I could use a cup of coffee though." Arie sat at the table, and Joey brought him a mug before sitting next to Robbie. "So what's the plan for today? Robbie said we were gonna swim, so I brought my suit."

Joey took a sip of his coffee. "Good. We'll leave as soon as we're finished here." They finished their breakfast and cleaned up before getting their things together and piling into Joey's car.

The ride took about half an hour as Joey drove them out toward Ludington State Park, stopping just outside the gate. "What are we doing?" Robbie asked as Joey parked the car, a slight hint of trepidation in his voice.

"There's a channel where the river meets Lake Michigan, and I thought we could swim in the flowing water."

Arie got out and walked toward the beach while Joey helped Robbie change into his bathing suit. "I don't swim," Robbie confessed. He seemed ashamed of the fact.

"Don't worry, I'll hold on to you the entire time." After changing into his own suit, he helped Robbie make his way across the sand and down to the water's edge before guiding him into the water. As they got farther out, the current swirled around their legs. As the water got deeper, Joey held Robbie close and let the water carry them along. At first Robbie was unsure, but Joey held him close and they rode the current toward the lake before walking hand in hand back up the beach and doing it again.

"Having fun?" Arie inquired as they began another trip down the river.

"We sure are." Robbie beamed as he and Joey rode the water together, laughing as they did. For Joey it was an incredible time. Every time they floated down the river, he got to hold Robbie close, their bodies pressing together. But the best thing was the grin on Robbie's face. He glowed just like he had the first time he'd climbed on a horse. Robbie's ability to get the most out of each new discovery, each new experience, made them new for him too.

"When's lunch?"

"Always thinking with your stomach, huh, Arie?" Robbie commented as Joey led him out of the water and back to the car.

They changed in the back seat and rode back toward town, talking and laughing. As he drove, Joey tried to put aside the trepidation that threatened to build inside him. This was his last day with Robbie and each hour that passed put him one hour closer to separation. Shaking his head and returning his attention to the conversation, he once again pushed those feelings aside, but he knew they'd grow more insistent as the day drew on. Parking on Ludington Avenue, he led them toward one of the restaurants, guiding a self-conscious Robbie inside.

As they sat down, Joey heard whispered comments and teeth clicking, the faces displaying the all-too-familiar pitied looks. But this time, to his surprise, he didn't really care. Robbie didn't see it, and the people who really mattered didn't care about his face, so why should he? For the first time, he realized that over the last two weeks, he'd been able to show Robbie all kinds of new experiences and at the same time, Robbie had given him something too: confidence. Robbie saw him as beautiful. He'd told him that often enough, and Joey was starting to believe it.

"I'm Carrie, can I get you something to drink?" their server said in her perky waitress voice. They ordered, and when she stepped away, Joey read Robbie the menu and helped him choose what he wanted. When she returned, they ordered lunch and then talked as they waited for their food.

"What time is your performance tonight?"

"We need to be there by seven-thirty," Arie supplied, "and the performance is at eight."

"Are you coming?" Robbie asked hopefully.

"I wouldn't miss it. What are you playing? I know you told me, but I can't remember." Their food arrived, and they waited until the server left before continuing their conversation.

"We're playing Beethoven's Ninth Symphony, with soloists and a local choir. It sounded great in rehearsal." Robbie commented between bites. "Man, this is good." He grinned as he took another bite. They continued talking, eating, and laughing, with Joey taking mental pictures of Robbie's smile and recordings of his laughter. After lunch, they made their way back to the car.

On the way back, they dropped Arie off and continued to the farm. Joey parked near the barn and helped Robbie inside. "I thought we'd go for a ride." Joey brushed Twilight and got her saddled before helping Robbie mount and then joining him.

Twilight knew her way to the creek without any guidance from Joey, which was good, because he was barely paying attention. His mind was on the arms around his waist and the soft breaths against his neck. Every part of him was keenly aware of Robbie's chest pressed to his back, hips pressed to his butt. Entering the wooded area, Joey slowed the horse, and they ambled on. At the creek, he turned the horse upstream until they came to a small clearing where he stopped the horse.

"Where are we?"

"At the most special place on the entire farm." Joey slid off and handed Robbie the reins. "I'll be right back." Robbie nodded, and Joey took the blanket he'd attached to the saddle and spread it on the ground before leading Twilight to a post and hitching her to it. Then he helped Robbie to the ground and led him to the blanket, both of them settling on the ground. "Geoff told me once that he and Eli first made love right on this spot." Joey loved this spot but he always approached cautiously because Eli and Geoff returned to it quite regularly. It was after Joey found them once that Geoff had explained why it was so important to them.

Leaning close he expected to make the first move, but Robbie beat him to it, putting his hands on his cheeks and kissing him hard and long. "I can feel how wonderful it is here—the rustle of the leaves, the gurgles from the stream, the tramping of Twilight's hooves, the scent of earth and blossoms. I bet it's beautiful."

Joey swallowed. How come this person who could see nothing could find such beauty around him? It just blew him away. "It is, but it pales next to you."

Robbie blushed and started to shake his head, but Joey kissed away his denial, pressing him back against the blanket. This was their last day together. Throughout Robbie's visit, they'd shared a number of firsts, but now everything they did was the last, and Joey was determined to make it the best.

Slowly, between kisses, he popped open the buttons of Robbie's shirt, slipping the fabric over his shoulders and down his arms. After that, their clothing seemed to disappear as if by magic. He couldn't remember how, and it wasn't important. All that mattered was the touch of Robbie's lips or the caress of his hand against his skin. His mind needed it, craved it, and he reveled in it.

Moving away from Robbie's kissable lips, he slid down his body, tongue circling peaked nipples before sliding down his stomach and farther. The long, hard length called to him and he didn't tease; they were both too far gone. Opening his mouth, he took Robbie deep, sliding his tongue along the ridge as Robbie moaned and writhed beneath him, making small needy sounds that only increased his passion. "Joey!" He warned him, but Joey ignored it. He wanted it, needed to taste this man, wanted to remember it for a long time.

When Robbie collapsed back on the blanket, Joey brought their lips together, kissing long and deep. "I want to remember this forever."

"Me too." Robbie wrapped his legs around Joey's waist.

"Are you sure?" Joey asked against Robbie's lips and received a deep kiss as an answer. With a wry smile he knew Robbie couldn't see, and he couldn't stop, he kissed him again and tongued his way down the smooth body beneath him. This time he didn't stop, lifting Robbie's legs, he watched his face as he slid his tongue farther, deeper, finding the most private part of him. As he swirled his tongue around the opening, Robbie opened his mouth, crying out in an eye-widening, silent, exclamation of joy.

"What are you doing to me?" He managed to moan between deep pants of disbelief. Instead of answering he returned to his small target, swirling and teasing the puckered flesh with fingers and tongue, Robbie gasping as he thrust deep.

Reaching into his pants pocket, he found a small packet and tore it open, sliding the condom on and then slowly, lovingly, pressed himself into Robbie's body.

The heat alone threatened to overwhelm him as he pressed deeper and deeper, filling his lover, as Robbie's small cries urged him on. Then they were joined, the heat from Robbie's core traveling through him, forging them into one being, their spirits connected.

He didn't want to move, but his body could take no more, and slowly he withdrew and plunged deep again, the pressure around him almost too much. This was Robbie, his Robbie. Regardless of whether they ever said the words, regardless of if this was the first and only time they were joined, this was his Robbie. If he had to let him go, so be it, but right now Robbie was his. Leaning forward, Joey kissed him hard, tugging on those luscious lips as he drove deep inside him, the look of complete ecstasy never leaving Robbie's face—and he knew Robbie felt the same way.

They moved together, their bodies and spirits coming together in the ultimate expression of love. If they never said it, they were expressing it, and both of them knew it. "Robbie!" Joey felt his voice break as his passion could no longer be contained. His head spun and the world narrowed to only the small clearing and the man he was loving in it.

He heard Robbie call out his name, and he felt him clench around him. He knew Robbie was coming, and that thought broke his last thread of control, and he climaxed as well, filling his lover.

He stopped, afraid to move, because if he did, it would break their connection—this would be over, and he wanted it to last forever. But everything ends, and slowly, reluctantly, he slipped from Robbie's body and reclined on the blanket, pulling Robbie to him, their kisses less intense, but no less special. "I don't want you to go." There. He'd said it. At least part of it.

"I know." Robbie slid his fingers through Joey's hair.

"Are you looking forward to going home?" He knew this was a completely unfair question, but he'd asked it anyway.

"Yes." Joey felt his heart clench, knowing he shouldn't have asked if he didn't want to know the answer. "I mean, it's home. It's the place I know best. But I'm going to miss you very much. This place is so special." Robbie stopped and then continued. "Because you're special."

Joey swallowed the lump in his chest. "So are you." Joey clung to Robbie, holding his naked body to his. "Very special." He couldn't bring himself to say anything more, even though the words were right on the tip of his tongue. Instead he sealed their lips together, holding that sweet body, mapping him with his hands, memorizing the smoothness of his skin, the soft hair, the soft moans he made whenever Joey did something wonderfully unexpected.

The warm breeze rustled through the trees and caressed them as they lay in the shade. Joey held Robbie, afraid to move and break the spell, so they lay there, spending their last afternoon together listening to the water and wind, Twilight munching grass nearby. The only thing that would make this better was if Robbie wasn't leaving, if they could do this every afternoon instead of just today. Quietly, Joey rolled onto his side and Robbie curled up to him, spooning him, an arm resting on his side, hand stroking his stomach.

Joey felt the tears well in his eyes, fueled by disappointment and a touch of self-pity. Since the accident he'd given up on finding someone to love the way Geoff loved Eli. He didn't think anyone would ever love him like that. But he had found it, and it tore him up to have it taken away. Sometimes life just wasn't fair.

ROBBIE lay in Joey's arms, dozing in the summer sun. Their lovemaking had been so tender, so beautifully erotic. It felt so naughty being naked outdoors, but Joey made it seem so naturally erotic. "We should get back, although I'd like nothing better than to spend forever right here with you." He heard the hitch in Joey's voice and knew what it was because he was feeling the exact same way.

"I know." Robbie began feeling around and then laughed. "I can't find my clothes."

"Then you'll have to ride back naked." Joey's soft chuckle made his body react yet again. He loved the sound of that voice. It was so sexy and warm. It went right to his groin every time. "Can you imagine the reaction if you rode up to the barn naked? I'd have to beat them off with sticks."

He slapped Joey playfully and then felt a hand slide down his butt. "I'll need my pants just so you don't get in trouble." His clothes were handed to him, and he reluctantly put them on. Everything… even something as simple as getting dressed, had an air of finality around it. Once he was done, Joey took him by the hand and led him to Twilight, where he got into position, and after Joey was ready, he mounted and got into what had quickly become his favorite position, hanging on to Joey as they rode. He heard a soft clicking, and Twilight began to walk, taking them back to the farm.

Entering the kitchen after helping unsaddle and feed Twilight, Robbie heard what sounded like both Eli and Geoff working in the kitchen. They seemed so happy together, and while he couldn't hear what they said to each other as they worked, he could hear the sound of occasional kisses and soft intimate conversations that he purposely ignored. "Dinner will be ready soon, and then we all need to get ready for tonight's concert."

Robbie heard a mug clink on the table in front of him. "Who of y'all are going?"

"Everyone. I got fourteen tickets. The hands are going, along with Geoff's aunts, Len, and Chris—we should be quite a crowd."

Robbie sipped from the coffee mug in front of him. It was wonderful and very touching that everyone wanted to listen to him play. "Do you know where Joey is?" After sitting down, he'd heard Joey's footsteps.

"I think he's talking with Geoff." A chair scraped the floor. "You know if you wanted to stay, you'd be welcome."

Robbie gulped as he set down his mug. "Thank you. It's not a matter of wanting."

Love Means ... NO Boundaries

"I know. We just wanted you to know that you're always welcome here." He felt a hand on his arm followed by a soft pat and then heard Eli get up and go back to work. "We've all become very fond of you, ya know." Robbie heard a swallow and the hesitation in Eli's voice.

Two weeks ago, Robbie never dreamed that going back to Natchez would be so hard. He'd been traveling for almost two months, and while it had been fun, the last two weeks had been life-changingly memorable and he didn't want it to end. He'd actually found love and had begun a truly honest dialogue with himself about who he was and what he wanted. Now he had to leave Joey, which caused a grapefruit-sized lump in his throat whenever he thought about it. And he needed to tell his parents that he was gay. He wasn't sure how they'd take it, but he did know they'd love him no matter what.

He took another sip from the mug as his phone rang. *Speak of the devil.* He answered the phone and spoke with his mother, only paying scant attention to what she was saying, and telling her what the plans for his arrival were. He hung up and got to his feet, walking confidently through the house and up the stairs.

ROBBIE stepped from the shower and dried himself carefully, making sure he didn't hit anything. He was quite good at knowing where he was in familiar surroundings, but he never took it for granted. Wrapping the towel around his waist, he made his way to the bedroom he'd used for the last two weeks. He was going home, and he should be excited to see his family after months away, but he wasn't, not really. Leaving Joey was going to be hard. He knew he had to go home, but he really wanted to stay.

In the room he felt around on the bed and found his clothes all neatly laid out and ready for him. He also found Rex, and it felt like

113

he was lying on his jacket. "Hey, boy." He patted the dog's head affectionately. "I need my jacket." Nudging his companion, Rex moved off his jacket and Robbie found him resettled next to the pillows. "Where are the kittens?" As if on cue, he heard them mewling as they climbed onto the bed. He should have known. They were never very far from their daddy.

Dropping the towel, Robbie began dressing, trying to concentrate on the task at hand, but finding it difficult. His throat was dry, his fingers fumbled, and he finally sat on the edge of the bed.

"Damn it." He didn't want to leave Joey. He missed his parents and his home in Natchez, but he knew he was going to miss Joey something awful. "Why can't things be easy?" He could hear Joey moving around in the room across the hall, and he thought about going to him. Instead he decided to get ready. Hoisting himself to his feet, he finished dressing, fastening his buttons before slipping on his jacket.

"You look so handsome." He hadn't heard the door open, but he was glad Joey was there, and he could almost feel his gaze raking over him. "Do you need help?"

"No, I've got it." Robbie fastened his tie and then felt Joey near him, taking his arm.

"I know you don't need my help." Joey supplied before Robbie could say anything. "I just want to touch you."

Robbie wanted the same thing. Their time together was becoming very short. He followed Joey to the stairs and descended them slowly. The house was completely still, and Joey caressed his cheek and kissed him softly. "Everyone will join us there."

Robbie figured they were giving them time alone. He pressed the button on his watch and the mechanical voice told him the time. "We should go." He'd taken two steps when his phone began to ring. With a huff he answered it. "Hi, Mama."

Love Means ... NO Boundaries

"Hello, honey." She didn't go on.

"Is there something you needed? We're running a little late."

"No, I just wanted to make sure you have everything." She began to ask a litany of mother questions making sure he hadn't forgotten anything.

"I've got everything all set, Mama. We have to go. I'll call you tomorrow from the bus." The last thing he wanted was her calling during their last night together.

"Okay, I'll talk to you tomorrow." Robbie could hear the excitement in her voice and knew she was looking forward to having him home.

"Is she okay?"

"Yeah, she's excited." Robbie wished he was. Then this wouldn't hurt so much. "Let's go." He said lightly to Joey, and they made their way out to the car.

Inside he buckled up and waited for Joey, who thunked the door closed and started the car. They didn't talk while they rode, but he felt Joey's hand on his thigh the entire time, and he kept his hand on Joey's, needing the contact.

Robbie felt the car slow and stop. Then the engine was silent, and he heard the car door open. He got out and felt Joey's touch on his arm, leading him toward the building, a steady stream of reassuring instructional patter flowing in his ears.

Inside the auditorium he heard Arie's voice, and then his friend was nearby. "I'll take him backstage. You have seats right down front."

Robbie held Joey's arm, not wanting to let go, but he finally released his grip. Joey handed him his case, and he let Arie lead him away.

"It's okay, Robbie," he heard Arie say as he was led down a hall, hugging his violin case to him like a security blanket. He felt a whoosh of air as a door opened, and he was led to a chair.

"What am I going to do, Arie?"

"You're in love with him, aren't you?"

Robbie couldn't speak, so he nodded his head slowly.

"That's good, because he's in love with you too."

"He hasn't told me." Robbie felt tears welling in his eyes.

"Have you told him how you feel?" Robbie shook his head as an answer. "Then how can you expect him to say something? You have a mouth, use it."

Robbie nudged Arie, and he felt a ghost of a smile come to his face.

"Besides, if the look I just saw is any indication, he feels the same way you do and probably has for a while."

"What do I do?" Robbie's smile faded and his misery returned.

"I don't know what you can do except make the most of what you have." The room around them became quiet as the conductor gave them last minute instructions. Then they tuned and warmed up before Arie took his hand and led him to the stage.

As he took his seat to applause, he listened carefully. "Robbie." The word was whispered but it sounded to him like a welcome bullhorn, and he turned, instinctively knowing where Joey was, feeling his gaze on him.

Robbie heard the applause again, and the orchestra tuned and became quiet before the applause started again, and the conductor entered. He waited and then heard the small tap and felt the tapping of the conductor's foot.

Love Means ... NO Boundaries

The first note of the symphony carried Robbie away. The music never ceased to fill him with awe. He felt a kindred spirit with this music. He's never seen it, only heard it. And Beethoven had only seen it on paper. He'd never heard it because he was deaf when he wrote it. That bit of irony bound Robbie to the piece.

As they moved through the first and second movements, he could feel an invisible connection, like Joey was linked to him and the music. After the second movement, they took a brief break and the choir and soloists entered, the risers behind them creaking and moving. Robbie felt his excitement ramp up.

The third movement began, lively and energetic, building toward the climactic final movement. As the music faded away, Robbie heard a whisper, one that went right to his heart. "It's beautiful." Joey had used that word enough that he'd know it anywhere.

The choir stood behind him and the fourth movement began. The "Ode to Joy" was one of Robbie's all-time favorites, and it never ceased to move him. As the piece built from the soloists, answered by the choir, up to the melodic climax, Robbie felt everything recede, the orchestra, the conductor, the voices, and his focus moved to the seat in the front row.

As he played like he'd never played before, the music swelled to a crescendo and the choir sang out loud and full, a song to joy, and Robbie's violin sang along with them. Echoing the blissful joy in the music, Robbie sent everything he had to Joey, all the joy, all the love, everything. This was his one and only chance. He gave it his all, and the orchestra seemed to understand, building and carrying his joy along with theirs, filling the space, and it seemed to Robbie as though every one of them was sending their joy to his Joey.

The music backed away and then built again to Beethoven's frantic, bombastic closing that echoed through the hall long after the music ended. Robbie breathed hard, gasping for breath as the final note drifted away, replaced by deafening applause.

He'd been playing for one person, and he heard something unique, a soft chant, "Robbie, Robbie." It wasn't loud, but he could hear his friends letting him know they were there. Robbie smiled and stood up, taking bows when Arie indicated before following his friend off the stage.

As soon as he made it backstage, he was engulfed in a bone-crunching hug as someone, he presumed Arie, took his instrument. "You were amazing!"

"Thank you." He didn't know what else to say, and his brain was barely functioning.

Robbie felt lips press to his and heard a few tuts in the background, but he ignored them as he was kissed within an inch of his life. And to think a few weeks ago, he was trying to accept who he was, and here he was being kissed in front of everyone, and he really didn't mind.

"You two go on," Arie chuckled behind them. "Here's your case, I'll look for you in the morning." Robbie felt Joey pull back slightly, but he didn't let him go. Then his case was placed in his hand.

"Thanks, Arie. You're a good friend." He really was, and since their talk, Arie couldn't have been more supportive. Robbie heard Arie mumble something about going already, and then Joey was nudging him away where it turned out a small crowd was waiting for them.

They talked for a while, laughing and going on about the performance before saying their good nights and filtering away.

"We should go home." The short ride was quiet, each of them engrossed in their own thoughts. Robbie felt the car pull off the road and heard gravel crunch under the wheels. "Could we stop by the barn? I have to leave early, and I want to say goodbye." The car stopped, and the engine cut off.

"Sure. When you get out, the barn door will be right in front of you."

Robbie stepped forward, feeling the concrete apron beneath his feet, and then the door rested against his hand. As he lifted the latch, the familiar smell came to him. He was going to miss that smell. "Hi, Twilight." He walked right up to her, feeling the long nose with his hand. "I'm going to miss you, girl. Thanks for all the fun and adventures."

He heard a breathy snort from across the way. "You feeling jealous, Tiger?" He moved toward the sound and felt a nose bump against his chest. This time he was ready for the horse's show of affection. "I'll miss you too."

"I think they all will. I know I'm going to."

Robbie felt the lump in his throat get larger, and he turned his head, listening to the sounds of the barn, impressing them on his memory as he inhaled deeply, the scent of fresh bedding and horses filling his nose.

Then he felt Joey next to him, holding him, lips pressing to his neck. "Let's go inside," whispered words reaching his ears. Then slowly, he felt himself being led out of the barn and into the house. Robbie heard soft voices in the house and it seemed as though Eli and Geoff were discussing something heatedly. He couldn't make out what they were saying, and the voices got softer as they made their way up the stairs and into Joey's bedroom. He heard the door click softly, and Joey's lips were against his, softly kissing, the intensity building.

"Joey, I want...." Joey was kissing him again and gentle hands began slipping the jacket off his shoulders, removing his tie, opening his shirt. Those hot, strong hands continued their work, not stopping until he was standing naked. Joey pulled away, and he heard rustling as fabric fell to the floor, followed by the chink of a belt and the thunk of shoes. Then Joey was kissing him again, hot skin pressing against his, warmth traveling all through his body as he was guided to the bed.

The kisses continued as he was positioned on the bed, Joey's hot body on top of him, moving against him. They rolled on the bed, and he was pressing Joey into the mattress. Robbie loved that Joey was willing to let him have control. It was one of the things he most loved and one of the things he'd miss most about him—Joey treated him as an equal.

Robbie felt Joey's legs circle his waist, and he knew what Joey wanted. They kissed as hands roamed, kissed as fingers explored and teased, kissed as cocks rubbed together, and kissed as Robbie pressed to Joey's opening and entered his body. Robbie pulled his lips away as he heaved for breath, sensations flooding his body.

Joey's hands tugged him back, returning their lips to what felt like their rightful place. "Take me, Robbie, I'm yours."

"And I'm yours." That was as close to a declaration as either of them could make, but it was enough for now, and Robbie nuzzled Joey's neck as he buried himself deep, the heat and pressure taking him. Then he heard something else, something new. His mind replayed the "Ode to Joy," and while this may not have been what the composer had in mind, it was the ultimate in joy for Robbie.

Suddenly, as they moved together, he heard himself humming it, sending the joy to Joey, and he heard it back. Soon they were moving together, their song, their joy, passing back and forth until neither could contain it any longer. They came, crying out each other's names.

As their passion waned, Robbie felt himself hugged to Joey, kisses placed on whatever skin was available, cheeks, shoulders, and lips. Robbie felt Joey stretch and a soft cloth passed over his skin. "I don't know what to say to you," Robbie confessed as he nestled in the crook of Joey's arm.

"Nothing to say, not now." He heard Joey's voice break, and he was hugged tighter.

Robbie let his hands wander over Joey's chest.

"What are you doing?"

"Sending a message to your heart not to forget me." His fingers beat a gentle staccato rhythm on Joey's skin.

"Is that Morse code?"

"Yeah, I learned it as a kid. Used to drive my mother and the maids crazy, sending messages to friends that they couldn't understand."

"I don't know what you're saying?"

"I know, but your heart does." Robbie kept up the soft tapping, repeating the message again and again. He kept up the soft tapping as Rex found them, jumping on the bed. He kept sending the message as the kittens joined them. He didn't stop until he fell asleep with Joey's arms holding him close.

Robbie woke to the sound of rain. *How appropriate.* Even the weather understood how he was feeling. He felt Joey stir as a soft buzzing sounded in the room. He didn't know what to say, and obviously Joey didn't either, because he held him tight even as others began moving in the house.

"Joey, Robbie." There was a soft knock on the door, "You need to get ready. You have to leave in less than an hour." Even Eli's voice reflected what they were feeling.

"Do you need help packing?" Joey got out of bed and Robbie felt his eyes on him.

"No, I'll be okay." He needed a few minutes to get himself together.

"I'll bring your clothes over to you in a few minutes."

Joey took his arms and pulled him into a kiss that had his head swimming. When Joey pulled back, he made his way to the door and across the quiet hallway to his room.

After dressing, he slowly and carefully put his things in his suitcase: his music sliding into the outside pocket, his clothes packed in a neat order. "You knew this was going to happen, but you fell in love anyway." He spoke to himself, trying to vocalize what he was feeling. But he knew he wouldn't change it, not now, not for anything.

Robbie heard the door open. "I've got your tux, and someone else came to say goodbye."

Rex jumped on the bed and Robbie patted him affectionately, getting licks and kisses in return. "You take care of those kittens." *Damn it.* The knot was forming in his throat again.

Taking the clothes from Joey, he continued packing as he heard Joey's footsteps retreat and return. "Robbie." Joey sounded as choked up as Robbie.

"Come with me."

"Stay with me."

They said together, each knowing that what they were asking wasn't possible, but they said it anyway.

"I know," they said in unison. Robbie had to go home. It was where his family was. His mother might be a pain and a little smothering, but it was home. And he'd never really ask Joey to give up the farm and his family here.

"What will you do when you get home?" Joey asked as Robbie finished packing. They'd never talked about anything that would happen after Robbie left. Neither of them had wanted to think about it.

"Hopefully, I can audition for a permanent place with a symphony." *Think about you. Wish you were with me.* Robbie closed his suitcase and zipped it closed. "Is there anything I forgot?"

He heard Joey move around the room. "No"

Joey picked up the suitcase and carried it downstairs.

Robbie followed after listening to the sounds of the house for a final time before making the trip through the now-familiar house to the kitchen.

"I know you have to go, but we'll miss you, and you're welcome here any time." He felt Eli give him a hug and step back before he was engulfed in another hug from Geoff.

"Take care and call us." *Damn, had he heard Geoff getting emotional?*

"I will."

They stepped back, and Joey led him to the car, placing his luggage in the trunk.

The car started, and Robbie felt it move, pulling out of the gravel drive and onto the smooth road, retracing the route they'd taken as strangers just two weeks earlier.

"Joey, I really wish I could stay."

"I know. It's okay. I wish I could go with you, but what would I do? I'm a farmer and this is what I know. And I know that you'd have no opportunities here. You need to be where you can make your music, and it isn't like you could do that here. I know all that. I'm just not happy about it." Robbie heard the hurt and frustration in Joey's voice. He was feeling the same way, but he just didn't see a way out of it.

"I'm sorry, Joey, maybe we should have talked about this."

"Maybe, but it wouldn't have changed anything. You'd still have to go home."

Robbie felt Joey take his hand, lifting it, lips brushing over his knuckles. "I'll miss you very much."

"Me too."

The car slowed and turned, pulling into the drive and stopping. He felt Joey lean close, kissing him gently. The words for what he was feeling almost came tumbling out, but he held them back again. "Will you call me?"

"As long as I get a good song on your phone."

Robbie pulled it out of his pocket. "You've already got the 'Ode to Joy'." Robbie ran his hand gently along Joey's cheek and felt him flinch slightly at the touch. "Remember, Joey, you're beautiful to me." He let his fingers wander over Joey's face: the smooth skin of his cheek, the stubble on his chin, his perfect nose and yes—even those scars that Joey hated, but were simply a part of the man he loved. He committed every bump and contour to memory.

As much as he didn't want to go, he knew he had to, so Robbie leaned close for a final kiss and opened the door, getting out of the car, retrieving his violin case from behind the seat. Robbie heard the trunk open and close and Joey's footsteps as he approached before guiding him toward the bus.

"Goodbye, Robbie." He found himself enveloped in a hug that he returned as vigorously as he received, saying his own goodbye in Joey's ear. He stepped back, and Joey helped him to the steps, and he climbed onto the bus.

Arie immediately guided him to a seat, putting his instrument in the overhead. The bus engine started and it began to move forward and turned. "Arie, do you hear that?"

Love Means ... NO Boundaries

"Sounds like a horn gone funny."

It is, but it's...." He listened, and it started again. It wasn't clear, but he could make it out. Dot, dash, dot, dot—L, dash, dash, dash—O, dot, dot, dot, dash—V, dot—E. Then it started again becoming softer as they drove away. Joey must have looked it up while he packed. "Arie, what am I going to do?" he asked, as he buried his face in Arie's shoulder, tears filling his sightless eyes.

Chapter 7

"Jesus, man," the tall, handsome, lanky blond groused as he climbed out of the water. "First you're too busy to spend time with me." He walked across the sand to where Joey was sitting. "I can understand that." The blond dripped water on Joey and that got his attention. "Hey, are you listening to me?"

"Sorry," Joey'd been lost in thought—really lost.

"You're always sorry." The blond put his hands on his hips in mock indignation as he continued. "As I was saying." His voice reflected attitude. "First you ditch me for two weeks, and I find out it's because you met someone, but this Robbie left a month ago, and you've been moping and a real drag ever since." He plopped himself on the towel spread next to Joey.

"I know, Lane. I'm sorry. It's just that I brought Robbie here, and I was remembering the great time he had playing in the water." Joey could almost see his smile as they'd floated together in the flowing water. "He said he couldn't swim, but I held him, and we floated and played in the water for hours. It was really special." For Joey, the feelings were just as fresh, just as raw, as the day Robbie left. Everyone, including Lane, kept telling him that he'd feel better with time and that he'd be able to get over Robbie, but it hadn't happened yet.

"I wish I had met him." Lane propped himself up on his elbows, soaking up the shade. Joey laughed as his friend—in Lane's words—shadebathed. He was so fair that any more than twenty minutes in the sun, and he'd be lobster red, so he pretended.

"I do, too, but if you remember, you were finishing your seminar in…." Joey crinkled his face. "What in hell was it, anyway?" Joey knew perfectly well what it was, but he got few opportunities to pick on Lane and this was definitely one of them.

"It was a literature class." Lane said indignantly and scowled.

"Come on, it was a naughty literature class." Joey covered his mouth with his hand, and he snickered into it.

"It was a great class that explored the history of erotic writing throughout various cultures." Joey saw Lane's eyes begin to light with mischief. "It was pretty fun and some of it was pretty hot." Lane smacked Joey on the shoulder. "So is he coming back?"

Joey shrugged, "I don't know; I sure hope so. I really miss him."

"You fell in love with him." Lane's statement would broach no argument. "Of course you miss him, but you need to move on with life. You've been holed up on the farm, working all the time, trying to avoid dealing with what you're feeling, and it isn't healthy."

Joey rolled his eyes. "Thank you, Lane Freud."

"I'm serious. You need to move on. How often do you call him?"

"Only once a week." Joey reclined on his towel, hoping Lane would get the hint and stop. He didn't.

"How often are you e-mailing him?"

Joey pretended he hadn't heard, but Lane wasn't about to give up, and Joey knew it. "A few times"—he peeked at Lane's face and saw his eyes drilling into him, waiting. Joey exhaled dramatically— "… a day."

"So you've been talking to him and calling him with no hope of seeing him. How do you expect to move on?" Joey knew Lane's reaction was out of concern, but it didn't make it any easier for him to take. "Joey, you know I love you, so I'm telling you this for your own good. You need to break off contact, at least for a while, and do your best to move on. You're only prolonging the pain."

Joey didn't know how to react. The last thing he wanted to do was give up. "I just don't know how I can." He rolled onto his side, looking at Lane. "How would you feel if someone you cared about just cut you off like that?" Joey knew he just couldn't do that.

"Well, you have to do something, because you can't mope around like you have been for the rest of your life."

The sun was getting really strong, and the shade that they'd been enjoying was quickly disappearing. Lane got to his feet and began gathering up his towel. "We should get back before I get burned, and aren't you helping Eli with one of his lessons?"

Joey reached for the shoe where he'd stashed his watch. "Damn, we'd better get moving. The class starts in an hour." Joey gathered up his towel and pulled on a pair of shorts before following Lane toward the parking lot.

The ride back to the farm was fun. They rolled down all the windows, cranked up the radio, and sang along, badly, with whatever happened to be playing. Lane was good for Joey. His optimistic attitude was catching, and for the first time in a while he felt almost normal by the time they pulled up beside the house. Joey climbed out and retrieved his things from the back seat. "I'll see you tomorrow, and we can go for a ride."

Love Means ... No Boundaries

Lane waved as he pulled away, and Joey went inside and changed his clothes, meeting Eli near the riding ring a few minutes before the start of his beginner's riding class. The ring behind the barn rang with the excited voices of Eli's students. Most of them were younger children, and Eli needed help getting them ready and just making sure they were okay through the class. This was also one of Joey's favorite classes because all the students were always so excited.

This group of students had just started a few weeks earlier, and when Eli had asked Robbie to help him, he'd been reluctant at first. A few of the kids had asked him what happened to his face, and he'd told them he'd been in an accident. Most of the kids, having their answer, went back to what they were doing, to Joey's relief.

However, Kerry, a small girl who had to be about five, had tugged on his pants leg, "Mr. Joey?" Her big eyes had looked up at him, and when he looked at her, she crooked her finger at him shyly, and he knelt down. "When I get hurt, my mama kisses it to make it better." She leaned forward and noisily kissed his cheek.

Joey had smiled at her. "Thank you, that helps."

She'd smiled back at him and skipped off to find her pony, while Joey just shook his head in complete disbelief and wonder. Out of the mouths of babes.

"Mr. Joey!" He turned to see Kerry running through the barn to get to her pony, which Joey had just finished saddling for her. How someone so small could fill the barn with her voice was beyond him, but she certainly did. "Is Strawberry ready?" Her face lit as he nodded and helped her mount the pony and walked her to the ring.

Eli was just starting to put the kids through their paces as Kerry got in line, and the lesson began. "Did you have a good time at the beach?"

He didn't have to look to know that Geoff was standing next to him. But while Joey was watching the students, he knew that Geoff's attention was focused on the instructor. "Yeah." He continued to watch the lesson. "It was nice to get away for a few hours."

"You've been working awfully hard the last month or so, not that you haven't always, but even more so the last few weeks. I don't want you working yourself to the bone." Joey turned and looked Geoff in the face. "Is there something you want to talk about?"

"Not really. It's nothing that talking's gonna help." Joey saw Geoff nod slowly and returned his attention to the lesson. After watching for a few minutes, he stepped into the ring and began working with a few of the kids who seemed to be having trouble. At least work and keeping busy kept his mind occupied. But the nights....

The lesson went really well, and the kids were all excited smiles as they dismounted. The older ones unsaddled their mounts and put their tack away while Eli and Joey helped the younger ones before making a check of the horses and heading toward the house. "Can I talk to you a minute?" Joey knew that look. He'd seen it often enough over the last month. Joey stopped and turned to Eli. Over the past month, everyone had wanted to talk to him about Robbie and everyone had an opinion about what he should do, but Eli was the only one who hadn't offered advice or asked him to talk about it.

Joey saw Eli's mouth twist into a slight smirk. "I know that you've gotten too much broken heart's advice from everyone over the last month, and I promise I'm not going to do that." Joey nodded and waited for Eli to continue. "You were on the farm when I first came here, so you know that I left for a while and returned to my family."

Love Means ... NO Boundaries

"I know. Geoff was heartbroken the entire time." Joey saw a touch of sadness flash across Eli's face and fade just as fast.

"What you don't know is the reason I came back. My mother sat me down and told me that she could see I wasn't happy and asked me why. I told her I'd met someone and that I'd left them behind to return to the community. That was the first and only time I ever saw anger in my mother's eyes. She told me that I was acting like a fool, that I needed to be happy and that she needed me to be happy. She told me that if living with the family in the community would make me happy, then that's what I should do. But—and I can still see her sitting in her chair, sewing something for one of my brothers—if I was staying for them or for my father and going to be miserable, then I was better off leaving."

Joey opened his mouth to say something, but Eli shook his head, and he snapped his lips shut.

"I'm telling you this because what my mother said to me also goes for you. If staying here will make you happy, then that's what you should do. But, if your happiness is tied to Robbie, then you need to be with him."

"That's just the thing. We were together such a short time. How do I know what I should do?" That was the real question for him. Was he making too much of a short, wonderful couple of weeks, or was Robbie the one?

Joey saw Eli smile knowingly and nod. "Then you need to find out for yourself." Joey watched as Eli turned and walked toward the house, leaving Joey alone with his thoughts.

"Are you saying I should move to Natchez?"

Eli stopped walking. "I can't answer that for you, but I can tell you that for your peace of mind, you need to find out." He took another step and stopped again. "And do it before the entire farm needs Prozac." Joey saw a huge grin just before Eli turned and walked into the house.

Instead of going inside as he'd planned, he veered off and walked around the house to the vegetable garden, standing at the edge of the large plot, looking over the straight rows of lettuce, carrots, beans, and cabbage before his eyes wandered to the patch of tomatoes that Robbie had planted. "He's right, I need to find out. But how?" Walking around the garden he continued thinking before walking back around the house and going inside.

Geoff and Eli were sitting at the kitchen table along with Len and Chris. They appeared to be waiting for something, and Joey was afraid it was him. "Joey, please sit down." Len indicated the chair next to him. Yup, it was him. Joey felt like an errant child who'd been called to the principal's office. "We're worried about you," Len started. "For the last month, you've been morose and extremely down, and we all just want you to be happy." Joey looked around the table and saw all four men nodding their heads before Len continued. "I know that you've been nursing a broken heart, but I think it's more than that."

The idea percolating in the back of his mind zoomed forward. "It is, and I've been thinking that I may need a vacation." Joey saw Geoff smile. "I need to make a few calls."

"I just need you back in time for haying in a few weeks," Geoff said, as Joey pushed back the chair and stood up. He suddenly felt an excitement and energy that he hadn't felt in weeks. He'd been going through the motions since Robbie had left and maybe it was time for him to take charge of something.

Taking out his phone, he dialed the number he knew by heart and listened for the ring. "Hello, Joey?"

"Hey, Robbie, can you talk? Is it a good time?" God, why was he feeling so... nervous?

Love Means ... NO Boundaries

"It's always a good time to talk to you. What's up?" He heard Robbie shifting around and imagined him setting aside his violin and bow.

"I was wondering if you have anything going on next week." Joey's stomach was fluttering with nervous excitement.

"No." He sounded guarded, tentative. Joey almost gave up, but plowed ahead anyway.

"Geoff gave me some vacation time, and I thought I'd come see you. That is, if it's all right with you."

"Of course it's all right with me." He could hear the excitement in Robbie's voice, and the image of his bright smile flooded his mind. "I'll arrange it with Mama. She hasn't said anything about having other guests, so it should be okay." Joey heard some of the energy fade from Robbie's voice, and he started to wonder if this was such a good idea.

"What is it?"

He actually heard Robbie's huge swallow through the phone. "Um, I haven't told them yet."

"Told them what?" Joey stopped. "That you're gay or told them about me?"

"Neither one."

"Maybe this isn't such a good idea." Joey wanted to hang up right away. He'd been such a fool for wanting this so badly. He thought Robbie felt for him, but now he wasn't so sure. "I'll talk to you later." Joey got ready to disconnect.

"No, Joey, don't hang up, please." Joey stopped and listened. "I want you to come, and I know I need to tell them." A deep sigh came through the phone.

Joey felt terrible. He knew he was putting Robbie on the spot and he didn't want to do that. He cared too much for him to put that kind of pressure on him. "It's okay. I'll just be a visiting friend."

"No!" Joey actually stepped back at Robbie's vehemence. "That's not fair to you. I need to tell them."

"Please don't do it for me." The words tumbled out as Joey felt flashbacks to his own coming out and the nervousness and angst he'd felt telling his mother, even though she'd already known anyway.

"I'm not. They deserve to know who I am, and they don't." Robbie's nervousness came through the phone.

"If you want, I'll be there with you."

"I think this is something I need to do." Robbie sighed softly. "Please come, I really want you to." The longing in Robbie's voice matched what he'd been feeling for the last month and it was that sound more than anything that convinced him that Robbie really did want him there.

"I want to too. I want to see you." Joey felt his leg start to shake. "I want to hold you again." He felt the emotions fell up inside, and Joey tried to keep his voice under control.

"Then you'll come?" There it was again, that same longing.

"Yeah, I'll come." Wild horses couldn't drag him away. Regardless of whether Robbie told his parents, he had to see him. His mind wasn't giving him any peace, and he knew he needed some form of resolution.

Putting his phone back in his pocket, he returned to the kitchen, finding four pairs of eyes looking at him, waiting. Joey broke into a grin, "Looks like I'm going south." All four faces answered with smiles, and then everyone got to work. They had arrangements to make.

Love Means ... NO Boundaries

ROBBIE sat in the shade of the front porch, every sound, every car that passed, making his heart beat faster. Joey was arriving today, and he was too excited to stay inside. He probably should have, the summer heat was oppressive, but he couldn't bring himself to do it.

Footsteps and the tinkling of glasses announced someone's approach. "Mr. Robbie, I brought you some cool lemonade." He heard the tray being set down next to him.

"Thank you." Robbie turned in her direction and gave her a smile. Adelle was an institution with his family. She and the gardener Raymond took care of everything—she inside and he outside. Growing up, they were some of his closest friends. Even as they got older, they never slowed and took such good care of him. "Would you sit with me?" He suddenly wanted some company.

"I can't, baby." He felt her touch his shoulder. "Your mama's having a brunch tomorrow for the ladies and I have lots to do." He felt her pat his hand. "You really should come inside. You'll cook yourself out here."

"I know, but...." He didn't know what Adelle thought about Joey's impending arrival, but her opinion suddenly seemed very important. "Are you okay with me being... you know... gay?"

"Sweetheart, if the young man you're waitin' on is the reason you've been so happy for the last week, I'll get down on my old knees and thank sweet Jesus for sending him to you." With that, he heard her walk away, and he smiled to himself before sighing softly. He wished everyone had been so understanding.

Robbie hung up the phone with Joey, a tingle of excitement running through him. Joey was coming for a visit! He barely had a chance to enjoy the feeling when he heard his mother's footsteps in the hall, and he remembered what he had to do. Picking up his violin from the cushion beside him, he located his bow and drew it across the strings, disappearing into the notes and rhythms.

He lost all track of time, which wasn't hard whenever there was music involved. Hours passed in the blink of an eye and only his sore arms and stiff neck reminded him it was time to stop. Placing the instrument in its case, he snapped the latches closed and heard the door open. "Are you done for the day?" The music room was the one place in the house that she never interrupted him. As long as he was playing, she left him alone.

"Yes, Mama." Joey stood up and walked slowly toward her voice. "What time is it? I left my watch in my room."

"Almost time for your father." The evening cocktail hour was a tradition that was never interrupted, and it started almost as soon as his father got home from his office and ended once Harriet served dinner. "I'll take you down." He felt a hand on his arm, and she led him through the big house.

Cocktails were served in what his mother called the parlor. Robbie remembered the room from before his blindness. He was sure that it no longer actually looked like anything in his imagination, but he had nothing to replace the picture with, so it stayed as it was for him. As he settled on the sofa, he heard the front door open and his father's footfalls through the hall, getting closer.

"Robert Edward, how was your day?" Robbie heard the tinkling of glass. "What would you like?"

"Whatever you're having will be fine." Robbie figured a drink would help steady his nerves. He usually just sat and drank a soda while his parents sucked down martinis and talked about their days.

"A soda will be fine." His mother corrected.

"Nonsense, Claudine, he's a man and old enough for a drink if he wants one."

Love Means ... NO Boundaries

Robbie felt a glass being pressed into his hand as his parents began talking the way they usually did, almost as though he wasn't even in the room. "I have something I need to tell both of you." Their conversation stopped, and Robbie wondered what was going through his parents' minds at that moment. "This isn't easy for me to tell you, and I don't know how you'll react, so I'm just going to say it." Robbie took a deep breath and took a gulp from the glass in his hand, the alcohol burning as it slid down. "I'm gay."

Robbie waited for the reaction, but the room remained nearly silent, with only the ticking of the clock in the corner filling the void. Robbie knew there was a ton of nonverbal communication going on between his parents—looks and gestures that he couldn't see. They could communicate silently to each other when they didn't want him to worry or know what they were feeling. Apparently they'd been doing it for years, but Robbie hadn't known about it until Arie told him about it a year ago.

Finally he heard his father, "Are you sure you're not just confused?" There was a softness to his voice he hadn't heard very often, not since before the illness, and the momentary warmth washed over him. He really missed that tone.

"I'm not confused, Papa. I may be blind, but I know what I feel and think." He tried to keep his voice level and use reason as opposed to letting his emotions rule the situation.

"But honey, how could you know if you can't see?"

He turned toward his mother's voice. "I just do, Mama. I know how I feel." He had to give them credit: they didn't yell or scream. Instead, they seemed to be trying to understand. "I know this is hard for you, but I've felt this for a while, though I haven't been able to face it in myself. It took me awhile to get up the nerve to tell you. I didn't want to lose you."

He heard his mother sniff softly. "Nothing you could do would ever make us stop loving you. We both love you very much, honey, *and we only want you to be happy. But this is a bit of a shock." She wasn't lying. He could hear it in her voice. He tried to imagine how his father was taking the news. The tinkling of ice in a glass indicated his father was having a bracer.*

"I know, Mama, but I wanted you and Papa to know who I was. I didn't want to lie to you anymore." He felt like a weight had been lifted off his shoulders. His parents were talking and listening. "There's more." He may as well get everything out in the open all at once. "At the last stop on the orchestra tour, I met someone. A boy named Joey."

He heard his mother's gasp. "Is he someone from that farm you were staying on?" Robbie heard the scorn in her voice. No one would be good enough for her son. "I knew I should have made you go with Arie." There were so many things wrong with that statement; Robbie didn't know where to begin, so he let her comment go as hurt feelings.

"It's all right, Claudine," his father soothed. "You've got some explaining to do, Robert Edward." The tone was harsher now, and the use of his full name meant he was in trouble.

Robbie pressed on trying to make them understand. "I know I should have told you sooner, but I wasn't ready to deal with it myself. I had to leave him, and this last month has been very hard. I've missed him terribly."

"You know it's more than you being gay. We can deal with that and accept that. You're our son, but being gay doesn't excuse you from family responsibility and proper behavior."

He did. The funny thing was that he hadn't been as nervous about telling his parents he was gay as he was telling them about Joey. He knew there was no way they were going to take it well.

Glasses tinkled as drinks were refilled, and Robbie figured both his parents had downed their drinks and were reaching for refills. "What will they say? I'll be drummed out." His mother was always given to the dramatic. "What will the U.D.C. ladies say when they find out that my son, my gay son, is dating a damn Yankee?"

"He may be a damn Yankee, but I think I love him!" That declaration, a surprise to himself as well as his parents, had the desired effect of stunning them into silence, and Robbie had never been more relieved for a dinner announcement in his life. As he got up from his chair, the glass he was holding was taken from his hand.

"We're not done with this discussion." Some of the anger had slipped from his father's voice, replaced with concern, and the knot in Robbie's stomach unwound slightly. He felt a hand on his arm, and they made their way to what he was sure would be a tension-filled dinner.

He wasn't disappointed. What little conversation there was happened between his parents and they pointedly avoided talking about his announcement. As soon as dinner was over, Robbie excused himself, and Adelle took him upstairs. He shut himself in his room where he immediately picked up the phone and called Arie for support.

"So you told them, huh? All of it?"

"Yup." He was actually proud of himself. He'd been honest with them and had told them the truth.

"So he's really coming for a visit?" Arie seemed pleased.

"He's calling tomorrow to tell me when to expect him. I hope they come around." Robbie couldn't contain his excitement. Telling his parents had lifted a weight off his shoulders and he felt free regardless of his parent's reaction.

"They will. They just need some time to come to grips with what you told them. It'll be fine, you'll see."

It took some convincing on Robbie's part, but his mother had indeed come around, at least to a degree. She was a mother, after all, and wanted her son to be happy. They'd talked quite extensively about him being gay, and while she was still working through things, she was trying. The Yankee part was another story.

"When do you expect him?" He knew his mother was exceedingly curious about meeting Joey. Robbie felt her hand on his shoulder, and he put his hand on hers.

"Thank you, Mama. I know none of this has been easy for you or Papa." He turned and looked in her direction.

She sighed softly. "I always looked forward to grandchildren." Her hand slipped from his, and he felt her sit down next to him. "Lord, it's hot." She shifted on the seat and remained quiet.

"What is it, Mama? What's got you scared?"

"I keep forgetting that you see things better than most of us." He heard her breathe deeply. "What did I do to make you... you know?" She couldn't say the word.

"Gay?"

"Yes. Was I dominating? Did I keep you too close to me?" Fear touched her voice.

"No, you did nothing wrong." Robbie turned toward her and felt for her hands. "I know in my heart that I was born this way. All those things you might have heard about dominating mothers and the rest is just crap." He felt her flinch at the mild expletive. Robbie's mama wouldn't say shit if she had a mouthful. "Sorry, Mama, but it's true. I know there are people who won't like that I'm gay, and you may pay the price." Robbie knew the "Daughters" could be a rabid bunch and were staunchly conservative, both in religion and otherwise.

"Don't you worry about it, sweetheart."

Love Means ... NO Boundaries

"I do, Mama." Robbie swallowed hard. "You shouldn't have to pay for who I am." He waited for her to say something, but hearing nothing, continued. "I was so nervous about telling you and Papa, and I appreciate how understanding you've been." He leaned next to her and kissed her cheek. "I love you, Mama."

"I love you too."

Robbie knew there was a lot behind her voice. He knew his mother wished he were straight, would get married, and have children to leave Wildwood to. He even suspected that both his parents hoped this was a fad that he'd get out of his system. He wasn't fooling himself that they fully understood. They wouldn't, not after such a short time. But they'd listened and were trying, that was all he could ask for. Hell, it was more than he thought he'd ever get. He was beginning to wonder if someone had made off with his mama. "What did the ladies say anyway?"

"I haven't told them." *Silly boy.* "And I don't intend to. And while your young man is here, I expect both of you to behave appropriately in public." That was the Mama he'd come to expect. "What happens behind closed doors is nobody's business, but what happens in public is everyone's business. I hope the boy has some manners."

Robbie smiled and waited for her to realize what she'd said.

"Not that you're allowed to do anything under my roof with that boy!" That was definitely the Mama he knew. He smiled at her and patted her hand indulgently. He had no intention of keeping his hands and other parts off Joey for an entire week.

A car pulled along the road and stopped in front of the house. He heard it move again and turn into the drive before pulling up in front of the house. Robbie felt his heart beat faster as his mind pulled up the picture he'd found in his mind. *Oh God.* He hadn't warned his mother.

CHAPTER 8

JOEY pulled the car to a stop in front of the address Robbie had told him and stared openmouthed at the house. He double checked the GPS he'd gotten with the rental car before returning his gaze to the house. "Jesus." Steadying his nerves, he pulled forward and turned into a circular driveway that was lined with lush flowers and trimmed with low, formal hedges.

Parking in what he hoped was an out of the way place, he got out and couldn't help staring up at the white-columned edifice with its first and second floor porches. His stomach did cartwheels, and he almost got back in the car to leave, feeling so very far out of his element. But he saw Robbie sitting on one of the chairs on the porch with a striking woman next to him who Joey thought had to be his mother. Steeling his nerves, he checked in the mirror to make sure he didn't look as poor and shabby as he felt. "Damn. His hair was fine, but the scars were all he could see. His only comfort was that Robbie knew and didn't care.

The heat assaulted him as he walked along the drive to the front steps, taking each intimidating one as though he were approaching a hallowed place. Then he saw Robbie clearly and had to stop himself from rushing to him. His entire body wanted to take Robbie in his arms, and he briefly looked down to make sure he wasn't displaying his excitement for all to see.

"Joey, is that you?"

"Yes, I made it." He smiled, even though Robbie couldn't see it.

Robbie stood up. "This is my mother, Claudine Jameson." She stepped forward, and Joey walked to her, taking her hand.

"I'm very pleased to meet you, Mrs. Jameson. Robbie has told me so much about you." Joey remembered to smile and tried to cover the butterflies that were beating their wings all to hell in his stomach.

"It's nice to meet you," she replied in her best formal Mississippi tone before motioning him to one of the empty chairs. "Would you like some lemonade?" He saw her look twice at him, but her face showed only polite interest.

"Thank you, ma'am, that would be very nice." Anything for some sort of relief from this heat.

She poured him a glass and refilled Robbie's before placing the pitcher back on the tray. "If you'll excuse me. Adelle will call you for dinner." She stood up to leave, and Joey put down his glass and stood as well. He had no idea where he'd learned that, but something told him to stand when a lady left the room.

Robbie's mother turned with a ghost of a smile on her lips. "You have manners, I'll give you that." She walked inside, leaving them alone, and Joey felt like he could breathe again and sat back down. He wanted to reach for Robbie, pull him into his arms, and kiss the breath out of him, but this wasn't the farm, so he restrained himself.

"Did you have a good flight?" Robbie looked edgy and stiff, and he didn't know what to make of it.

"It was fine. But long, way too long." Everything had seemed to move in slow motion since he knew he was coming. He'd thought about seeing Robbie for the last month, and now that he was here, he didn't know what to do.

"Would you like to go inside? It's awfully warm, and I was only sitting out here waiting for you."

Joey sighed with relief. "Thank God, I've never felt heat like this."

Robbie smirked. "Even when the air conditioning went out on the tractor?"

"At least I could open the windows."

Robbie laughed and got up, carefully making his way to the door. "Get your things and we can take them up to your room."

My room. Joey felt a momentary stab of disappointment. He realized he'd been expecting to stay with Robbie the way they had on the farm, and that wasn't practical or realistic.

Joey got his suitcase from the trunk and met Robbie at the door, letting him take his arm as they went inside.

The air conditioning felt amazing as they passed indoors, and Joey stopped, his mouth hanging open, taking in everything. The house had been grand on the outside, but inside it was palatial, with gleaming wood, sparkling crystal, rich carpeting, and painting-covered walls.

"Is something wrong?" Robbie asked.

"No." Joey took Robbie's arm again. "I've never seen anything like this before. It looks like a museum."

"I wouldn't know. All the rooms look to me like they did ten years ago when I lost my sight, and the images get dimmer with time."

Doors were open, and Joey peeked into a beautiful living room as they made their way to the grand staircase. The dining room, with its rich walls and gleaming table, caught his eye, and Joey felt so intimidated.

He kept looking around as he guided Robbie up the stairs to the landing. "Your room is the first one on the left." Robbie pointed to the room with the open door, and Joey went inside, hoping Robbie would follow.

The bright room was huge with a sitting area and an antique bed. Guests were made very welcome by Robbie's family. Gingerly, Joey set his suitcase by the bed and looked around, afraid to touch anything. "It's just a house, Joey." Robbie stepped in the room and closed the door with a snick.

Joey took that as an invitation, moving quickly to do what he'd wanted since he'd arrived. His arms enveloped Robbie, and his lips found their companions. The sweet taste and supple softness was exactly as he remembered. His tongue stroked along the edge of those incredible lips, releasing what he'd been missing. And he heard it, that soft whimpery moan Robbie made that shot bolts of desire straight to his groin.

Joey felt Robbie hold on to him, steadying himself as Joey's mind clouded with unadulterated need.

"Joey," Robbie whimpered softly against his lips, "we need to be careful," before resting his head against Joey's chest, hugging him close.

"How did your parents take the news?"

"That I'm gay? Much better than they took the news that you were a Yankee."

Joey had to stop himself from stepping back in surprise. "That attitude still exists?" It was hard for him to fathom. To him that type of thing belonged in another time.

"Oh yeah, it still exists."

Joey just held Robbie, enjoying having him in his arms again, feeling the warmth against him, the scent of his clean skin. "I missed you," he whispered into Robbie's ear.

"Yeah, what did you miss most?" There was a playful sparkle in his words.

"Your voice, the way you turn one syllable words into two." Joey leaned close, running his tongue along the base of Robbie's neck. "The way you shiver whenever I kiss you right there." He ran his thumb across Robbie's lower lip. "The way this trembles whenever you come." Joey captured the lip in question, tugging gently until it pulled free.

"Did you mean it? The message when we were on the bus— that was you, wasn't it?"

"Yes, I meant it. I wish I'd told you sooner, but as you got on the bus, I found the sheet in my pocket I'd printed earlier to try to decipher what you were telling me, and I realized I couldn't let you go without telling you how I felt. I wasn't sure you'd understand it, but I had to try."

Before he could say more, they heard a soft knock. Robbie stepped back as the knob turned and the door opened. "Mr. Robbie, dinner will be ready in half an hour. You should get dressed."

Joey saw the petite, dark-skinned woman step into the room. "Thanks, Adelle. This is Joey Sutherland."

A smile broke out on her face, making her suddenly appear beautiful. "So this is the young man you were so excited about. It's nice to meet you. Mr. Robbie has told me a lot about you." She turned back to Joey. "You two better be careful, your mama's got everyone watching you like a hawk." Her expression softened. "Don't you worry yourself on my account." Joey watched her look to the door before shutting it and reaching into her apron and pressing something into Robbie's hand before opening the door again. "Just be quiet tonight." Once the door closed, Robbie felt in his hands and smiled, holding up two skeleton keys.

"What did she mean, dress for dinner?"

"Mama insists that dinners be special, particularly when Papa's home."

Joey felt the butterflies again. "I don't have anything fancy to wear." He was so out of his element.

"A shirt and tie is fine. You can borrow one of mine if you need to."

"I'll be okay." He'd wear his best, and if that wasn't good enough, or if they were that snooty, then too bad. He was here to see Robbie, not be all fancified.

"I should go change."

Joey captured his lips again and then watched as Robbie opened the door, feeling his way across and down the hall. Joey peered out the door, confused at Robbie's behavior. He'd been so confident at the farm, moving about easily. Easing back inside, he closed the door and opened his suitcase, getting out his good clothes.

Cleaned up and changed, Joey checked himself in the mirror. He had a plain-colored shirt, and he'd changed his jeans in favor of a pair of light dress pants. He hoped he didn't have to dress like this every night, or he'd be wearing the same pants every time.

As he looked at himself, he noticed that the scars had indeed begun to fade. Looking at himself wasn't something he did all that often, and he noticed that many of the once pink lines were now fading to white and in some places beginning to disappear, just like the surgeon said. Shrugging, he tied his plain-colored tie, and after making sure it was straight, opened the door. Robbie's was closed, and thinking he'd already gone down, Joey walked to the stairs.

There was no one in the dining room, but the table had been impressively set. Shoving his hands in his pockets, he followed the sound of tinkling glassware and saw Claudine and a tall, broad man who had to be Robbie's father.

"You must be Joey," the man pronounced as he poured a drink and handed it to Claudine. "Would you like one?" he held up the pitcher.

"Thank you."

He poured the drink and set down the pitcher. "Robert Edward Jameson." He held out his hand, and Joey shook it firmly.

"Joseph Sutherland. Everyone calls me Joey."

"It's good to meet you." He handed Joey the martini glass. Joey kept looking for some sort of joke or sarcasm, but saw none.

"Where's Robbie?"

"I thought he'd already come down." Joey looked surprised. "His door was closed." Her reaction seemed puzzling.

"You didn't bring him down with you?" She seemed concerned. "I'll call Adelle." She sounded miffed, and Joey wondered what he'd missed.

"Why does someone need to bring him down?" Joey took a sip of the drink and nearly choked. He must have merely waved the vermouth over the pitcher. *Damn that was strong.*

"He's blind." She looked at him like he was completely stupid and left the room.

Joey didn't know how to react, but something wasn't right. "When he was at the farm, he got around the house with ease. The barn too," Joey tried to explain.

Love Means ... NO Boundaries

"I knew it." Joey stopped himself from smiling at the accent as Robbie's father sat down in one of the wing back chairs. "She insists on doing everything for him instead of letting Robbie do things for himself." He sipped his drink and sort of shrugged, looking like it was a fight he'd fought before and didn't want to get into again.

"Do you think I talk funny, boy?"

Joey mustn't have been as good as he thought at regulating his expression. "No, but I bet you think I do." Robbie's father slapped his leg with a burst of laughter.

"A sense of humor, I like that." He took another sip and motioned to a chair. "Sit down."

Joey did as instructed, sitting rigidly in the chair, wondering what he should say and deciding he should say nothing and try to keep from spilling on himself.

A few minutes later, Claudine returned with Robbie on her arm. Joey stood and gave his chair to her, sitting on the sofa next to Robbie, while Claudine shot daggers at him. This was going to be a fun dinner. He just hoped he'd get a chance to explain.

Joey made a note to ask Robbie what was going on later. Robbie's father must have noticed the tension and started asking about his flight, making small talk.

"I understand you live on a farm."

Joey loved the man's accent. "Yes, sir. We have over two thousand head of cattle and almost three thousand acres, as well as horses."

"What is it you do on this farm?"

Joey knew he was being politely grilled, so he remained calm and answered in as even a voice as he could. "I manage the acreage we plant in corn, hay, soybeans, and alfalfa."

"How much is that?"

"About nine hundred acres." Robbie's father seemed impressed. "After I graduated from college, Geoff and Eli offered me a job." Joey shifted on the sofa and felt Robbie's leg against his. The little touch was reassuring.

"They own the farm?" The looks passing between Claudine and Robert were fast and subtle.

"Yes, sir. Geoff inherited the farm from his father. It's been in his family for generations. He and Eli have been together almost six years now." Joey let a touch of pride show in his voice. He was proud of the farm and his friends, and he was going to show it.

Before any more questions were asked, Adelle stepped in the room and caught Claudine's eye before leaving again. "Let's go in, shall we?"

Joey took Robbie's arm—he wasn't going to risk Claudine's wrath again—and guided Robbie into the dining room.

Dinner, from Joey's point of view, was a little strange. The conversation, what there was of it, was pleasant enough thanks to Robbie's father, but Claudine sat across from him and didn't waste an opportunity to stare at him. At first Joey thought she was staring at his scars, but he realized she just wasn't happy with him at all. She talked during dinner, but said little to Joey, just enough to be minimally polite, and Robbie said almost nothing. He simply ate slowly and paid no attention to anything. Granted, most of what was happening was visual and completely lost on him.

After what felt like hours, they got up from the table, and Robbie said good night to his parents, and to Joey's relief, Robbie asked him to take him upstairs. Joey was exhausted and uncomfortable to say the least. After traveling and the dinner table stare-off with Claudine, he'd had enough and just wanted to go to bed. Or more specifically, he just wanted to be in bed with Robbie in his arms, but he wasn't sure that was going to happen.

Love Means ... NO Boundaries

Joey left Robbie at his door, checking the hall quickly and then kissing him softly before going to his own room. Joey looked through the room, feeling more and more uncomfortable. Opening his suitcase, he pulled out a pair of comfortable shorts and a T-shirt. Pulling off the dress clothes, he folded them and put on the comfortable clothes and flopped down on the bed, his mind racing, going in circles. *I really shouldn't have come.* They'd had a wonderful time at the farm, but the Robbie he'd known there wasn't the same Robbie in the room across the hall.

Sitting up, he let his feet dangle off the bed while he thought. He knew what he needed to do. He didn't belong here, and he was just going to make things difficult for Robbie. In the morning, he'd call the airline, change his flight, and go home. With that settled, Joey turned off the light.

Then he heard it, the soft mellow tones of Robbie's violin. He'd heard Robbie play many things, but never something like this. It sounded like funeral music: slow, low, and sad, very sad. Like a moth to a flame, the music drew him across the hall, and he pushed the door open. Robbie was sitting on the edge of his bed, playing softly, tears running down his cheeks. His playing was always a window into what Robbie was feeling, and this was no exception. "I didn't think I could feel worse than when that bus drove away." Robbie hands stopped, but the bow remained against the strings.

Joey closed the door and sat on the bed, next to Robbie. "It's all right."

Robbie put the violin down. "No it's not. You're miserable. I don't have to see you to know that. I bet my mother stared at you all through dinner." Robbie shifted slightly on the bed. "I wouldn't blame you if you ran screaming from the house."

Joey reached for the instrument, taking it gently from Robbie's hands and setting it in its case. "I won't lie to you, I thought about leaving. I don't belong here, and your mother hates me."

"But my dad likes you, and that says a lot." Robbie leaned against him resting his head against his chest. "I missed you so much." This was why he'd come all this way, and Joey felt his resolve begin to crumble. Robbie angled his mouth toward his and that was it. One touch of his lips, and Joey knew he'd suffer the stares of an army of mothers for Robbie. He deepened the kiss, his tongue tracing Robbie's lips, tasting his sweetness. Robbie moaned softly.

A knock on the door broke them apart, and Joey groaned as Robbie backed away. The door opened, and Claudine glided into the room. "Do you need anything before bed?" Her eyes drifted to Joey and lingered for a second before returning to Robbie.

"No, I'm fine." Robbie reached to his mother and kissed her softly on the cheek. "I'll see you in the morning."

Joey saw her eyes drift over to him again, watching how close he was sitting to Robbie. Instead of letting it go, Joey took Robbie's hand, holding it in his. He saw her expression shift, but she said nothing and left the room. "I should get ready for bed too." Joey leaned to Robbie, taking his head in his hand and bringing their lips together. Joey wasn't subtle. He quickly deepened the kiss, devouring Robbie's lips and feasting on his mouth. He purposely made no further move other than to kiss him with everything he had.

Soft, throaty moans reached his ears and he kept on kissing. Joey knew he was driving Robbie crazy, and he could feel him trying to move closer, but Joey held him still and kept kissing. Then he pulled back, tugging Robbie's lower lip as he did. When the sweetness slipped away, he brought his lips to Robbie's ear. "Good night." He forced himself to get off the bed and quietly left the room. He wasn't sure if he was doing the right thing, but he needed Robbie to be the one to decide what else, if anything, happened.

Opening the door, he stepped into the hall, turned toward his room, and saw Claudine standing at the end of the hall looking like she was watching their doors, but trying to look like she was just

Love Means ... NO Boundaries

entering another room. Joey nonchalantly raised his hand and nodded before entering his room and closing the door. He had no doubt that if he hadn't left Robbie's room, they'd have gotten another, probably more forceful, knock on the door.

He hoped Robbie would want to join him, although he wasn't sure how that was possible with Officer Claudine watching their rooms, but he wanted Robbie in his arms more than he'd wanted anything in his life. Kissing him and then backing away had been nearly impossible, but the decision had to be Robbie's. After cleaning up, he got undressed, turned out the lights, and climbed in the bed.

He couldn't sleep. His mind wouldn't shut off, and his body screamed for Robbie. It knew he was so close and yet so distant. Lying on his back, Joey stared at the ceiling, listening to the sounds of the house, wishing Robbie was there with him. He heard footsteps in the hall. He even heard someone stop outside his door, and he hoped it was Robbie, but whoever it was moved on. Joey tried to sleep, but there was no way.

The house became still, and the light under his door flicked out, and still no Robbie. Resigning himself to a night alone, he rolled over and punched the pillow, trying to will himself to sleep. It wasn't working.

ROBBIE didn't know what to do. He'd been lying on his bed for hours trying to decide what he wanted. The house had become quiet, and it had been hours since he'd heard a peep outside his door. Twice he'd gotten up and felt his way to the door, only to make his way back to the bed. Throwing back the covers, he got out of bed, felt the top of the nightstand for the keys Adelle had given him, and made his way to the door yet again. He heard nothing as he pressed his ear to the door.

As he turned the knob, the door creaked softly, but it sounded like thunder to his sensitive ears. Again he stopped and listened. He heard nothing. No one asked him what he was doing, so he stepped out into the hall and closed the door. Inserting a key in the lock, he tried turning it and swore softly under his breath; then he used the other key to lock the door. He turned and shuffled across the hall to Joey's door, hoping it was unlocked. The door opened easily, and he stepped inside.

"Robbie, is that you?" he heard Joey whisper through a yawn.

Before he could answer, he heard footsteps and arms wrapped around him, lips taking his. This was what he'd wanted all those hours, and now he wasn't sure why he'd waited. "I hope so, or you'd be kissing my mother." Robbie began to giggle softly, and Joey silenced him with more kisses.

"We have to be quiet." Robbie felt himself being moved and then felt the mattress against the back of his legs. As Joey lowered him down, he heard a small creak and stopped. They moved again and another small creak followed. "Jesus!" Then Joey tugged him off the bed. "Just a minute."

The room filled with the sound of rustling fabric and Joey moving all around him. He couldn't figure out what was happening, but Joey seemed everywhere. As soon as he got a fix on him, he'd be somewhere else. "Joey."

"Shhh." A finger touched his lips. "Just a minute." He felt lips touch his neck, and he shivered for a second. Then they were gone again. *Fump. Fump.* Robbie turned toward the noise, but now everything was quiet. "There. Give me your hand."

"What are you doing?" Robbie felt hands slide down his chest and over his hips, boxers sliding down his legs.

"You won't need those."

His cock sprang free as the fabric slipped away, and he stepped out of them as he felt Joey kissing him again, guiding him down toward the floor. At first he wondered what Joey was doing, but then felt blankets and pillows, and finally a naked Joey sliding against his skin. "We need to be very quiet."

Robbie heard Joey snicker against his neck. "I'm not the one who yells."

He wanted to protest, but Joey cut him off with a powerful, mind-numbing kiss, and whatever he wanted to say flew from his mind. Hands glided over his skin, and Robbie began moaning uncontrollably. Every time he did, Joey kissed him harder. Hands slid over him and Robbie let his own do the same, gliding over Joey's back, reaching around to grab a handful of his work-hardened butt. "Joey, I want you." Robbie rolled beneath Joey and felt his lover splay himself on top, twisting his head so they could kiss.

Lips tasted his and then slid along his shoulders and down his back. Goosebumps raised on his skin as Joey continued his kissing, sliding down his body. When Joey reached his butt, Robbie buried his head in a pillow to keep from crying out. And when his cheeks were parted, and a hot tongue slid along him, delving deep, he cried out into the feathers.

Lifting his face away briefly, he gasped for breath as a wet tongue prepared him and a slick finger breached him, before burying his face in the pillow once more. His hips lifted of their own accord, and Robbie began whimpering as Joey found the magic spot inside him. Back and forth, he felt his hips grinding into the bedding. He tried to give warning, but when Joey's tongue took him deep, he came in a flash that sounded louder than a Beethoven finale and collapsed limp on the floor.

Robbie swore that Joey kissed every inch of his back and rolled him over and kissed his front from head to toe. Nothing was missed, and when Joey lifted his legs, Robbie pulled their lips together, and they kissed as he felt Joey slowly fill him. He couldn't see him, but he could feel Joey's breath as his own heart pounded in his ears. "Joey, more." His body was throbbing again, and he breathed frantically as Joey moved inside him. *Faster, harder, faster, harder.* A mantra formed in his head, and he wanted to scream it, but Joey seemed to know, because whatever he told himself he wanted, Joey did. The pressure inside his head built until he couldn't contain it any longer. Robbie had to shove a fist between his teeth to keep from shouting his happiness as he climaxed for a second time while Joey throbbed deep within him.

Joey hugged him close as he slipped from inside him. He was being kissed and loved, fingers gliding gently, softly over his skin. "Was that okay?" He heard the words, moaned softly as Joey nibbled on his ear. "I didn't hurt you, did I?"

"That was wonderful." Robbie found Joey's cheeks, stroking the stubbly skin. "You were wonderful."

Joey gathered him into his arms, their legs entwining, a blanket cocooning them in warmth. "I'm so glad I'm here."

"Me too." Robbie began to fall asleep, his mind closing. "I love you, Joey." Robbie heard an "I love you too" uttered in hushed, sleepy tones, and it was the sweetest music he'd ever heard, especially since it was punctuated by Joey pulling him close, spooning himself to his back as lips glanced over his shoulder. Then the room became very still as Joey's breathing evened out, and Robbie quickly followed him into dreamy sleep.

A sound on the edge of his mind penetrated Robbie's dream, and he started awake when he realized it was the sound of the hinges creaking as the door slowly opened.

"Mr. Robbie," whispered into the quiet room.

"Adelle?" he asked, as he felt Joey jerk awake next to him.

"Yes, it's me, baby." He heard footsteps, and then the door closed again, and Robbie felt something soft slip over him. "You need to get back to your own room before your mama wakes up." Robbie began to move and felt a hand on his shoulder. "I'll be right outside, and I suggest you put some clothes on. I don't need to be seeing your bits and pieces, now do I?" He heard her soft chuckle as she walked back to the door and a long, low creak as she opened the door and closed it again.

"Morning." Robbie was immediately drawn into a close hug as lips found his and his mind shut down. The kiss softened and faded away. "You need to get to your room."

He heard Joey get up and begin walking through the room. "Are you trying to get rid of me?" he asked, semi-seriously.

Suddenly the footsteps stopped for a second and then skittered closer. "Of course not, but I heard Adelle, and your mother already thinks I'm the devil incarnate."

"Well, you are a devil." Robbie smirked as Joey handed him his boxers, and he slipped them on and stood up. He heard a low growl and then a blanket was draped over his shoulders. "She's seen me before."

He heard the growl again and felt Joey pull the blanket closed around him. "You getting all possessive on me?"

"You bet your sweet ass!" He felt Joey squeeze his nether cheeks and then help him to the door. Robbie opened it and heard Adelle say something to Joey, and then his hand was taken, and he was practically dragged across the hall and in to his room.

"I thought you gave me your keys."

She humphed softly, "I gave you your mama's keys. What do you think I am, daft?" Her teasing tone told him she wasn't offended. "Git yourself dressed, and I'll be back as soon as I help that boy of yours put things to rights."

"Thanks, Adelle." He squeezed her hand and then let it go. Hearing his door open and close, he dropped the blanket on the bed and made his way to his bathroom. When he turned off the water and stepped out of the shower, he heard movement in his room and then quiet. Wrapping a towel around his waist, he finished cleaning up, putting everything back in its exact place and went to get dressed.

Robbie felt along his bed as he moved to his dresser and noticed that the blanket was gone and his bed made. He also felt that his clothes had been laid out for him. Adelle—she took such good care of him, yet was always so careful not to do too much for him. Just like Joey.

The familiarity and predictability were comforting for him, and he smiled as he dropped his towel and began pulling on his clothes.

He'd just finished dressing and was hanging up his towel when he heard a soft knock and his door opened. "Are you ready? Adelle said she has breakfast for us." Joey was suddenly very close, and he could feel his heat going right to him, his pants becoming a little tight. He made a note to make sure they woke up earlier next time.

"Let's go, I'm starved," Robbie leaned into the heat in front of him, "for more than food." He let his hand run down Joey's front, feeling the hard length he found in his pants and smiled as he stroked slowly.

"You're mean, particularly since your mother is coming down the hall." Robbie's hand snapped away, and he jumped back, almost losing his balance. Joey steadied him and then took his hand as his mother's footsteps approached. He'd know them anywhere. They stopped outside his door and then continued on. He felt so naughty holding Joey's hand in front of his mother, but he didn't pull away.

"Morning, Mama." She mustn't have heard him because she didn't answer, and then he heard footsteps on the stairs.

"Shall we?" Joey's voice sounded strange, but Robbie didn't know what to make of it, and he let Joey lead their way to breakfast.

Love Means ... NO Boundaries

"What did you have planned for today?" Joey inquired as he felt the top step.

"I don't really know. What would you like to do? I'm not much of a tour guide, for obvious reasons." He continued slowly down the stairs.

"I just want to spend the day with you." The sounds of dishware clinking reached his ears as they reached the landing.

"Why don't I call Arie and see if he could show you around town?" He felt Joey stop moving. "What?"

"I came here to see you, not spend time with Arie while you sat at home." His voice sounded so firm. "I came to see you."

Joey's vehemence was nice, and Robbie found that he liked being the center of Joey's very welcome attention. Truth be told, he figured Joey would leave for the day to look around, and he wouldn't see him until later. "Then I'll ask Arie if he'll show us around." Robbie figured he could go along if it made Joey happy, and it might be fun.

His smile lasted through breakfast as he and Joey ate in the kitchen. Adelle informed him that his mother had a U.D.C. meeting and had already left.

"She'll be gone most of the day, then?"

Adelle humphed as dishes clanked in the sink. "She'll have her meeting; then they'll go for lunch. She won't be home until her cocktail hour." Robbie smiled and felt Joey squeeze his hand as he heard Adelle mutter. "That woman never misses her cocktails."

"Adelle, would you sit for a while? You're making me jumpy, working while I'm sitting."

"Mr. Joey, I got work to do."

"I'll help you if you'll sit with us awhile."

Robbie heard a chair scrape the floor and a thump of a mug tapping the table.

"Thank you."

He heard Adelle laugh, "You Yankees is weird."

Both he and Joey began to chuckle, and Robbie felt like he should explain, but Joey beat him to it. "On the farm, we all help each other."

"Who does the cookin' on this farm?"

Robbie began to eat and listened as Joey answered. "Eli does most of it because he's the best cook, but we all take turns, and we all help clean up. Except whenever it's Geoff's turn, then we always end up in town."

"Who's this we?" Adelle seemed fascinated.

Robbie kept eating, steadily and gingerly so he wouldn't make a mess for Adelle to clean up.

"Geoff and Eli. It's their farm, and I live with them." Joey went on to explain. "Geoff is sort of like a big brother." Robbie heard Joey's fork against the plate, and Joey said, "This is really good, Adelle."

He heard her laugh outright. "You sure can put it away." Everyone was quiet until Adelle added, "I didn't mean nothin'. I like it when people eat—it means they appreciate my cooking."

"I sure did," Joey said. Robbie knew that Joey was really winning over Adelle.

"You two finish eating and don't you dare get up. I got work to do. Maybe I'll be making some of my fried chicken for dinner."

Robbie couldn't suppress a smile if he tried. "Her fried chicken is the best in the state, I swear."

Love Means ... NO Boundaries

Adelle made a pffft sound, but Robbie knew she was pleased. "You two run along now and have some fun. The quiet won't last forever."

Arie was thrilled that Robbie had called and quickly agreed to take them to see the sights. So, half an hour later they were ready, he and Joey waiting on the porch. Robbie heard a car pull up and Arie's laugh as he got out of the car. "Well, don't you two look sweet together?" He felt himself blush like a girl and felt Joey slink his arm reassuringly around his waist.

"I think we do." Joey's voice was full of confidence.

"Come on, lovebirds, let's get going." He felt Arie's hand on his arm as he was guided to the car. "Do you have your cane?" Robbie patted his side where a small leather pouch was attached to his belt. "Good. You probably won't need it because we'll be there, but...." Robbie heard Arie's voice trail off as the car door opened, and he felt his way into the back seat. "Why don't you get in with him, I don't mind playing chauffer."

"Thanks, Arie." Robbie really appreciated his friend's thoughtfulness. He heard doors close and felt Joey settle on the seat next to him as the car started and blessedly cool air began pumping from the car vents.

"I thought I'd drive you through town and let Joey see the historic district; then I thought we could take a cruise on the Natchez riverboat." Arie loved playing tour guide, and Robbie felt Joey vibrating with excitement.

For the next hour, they drove through town, Arie narrating the sites, explaining the history of the town and some of the homes, with Joey bouncing on the seat next to him like a kid. Robbie was so glad he'd come. Joey's excitement was catching, and even though he couldn't see any of what was being discussed, he could feel it through Joey. "When does the steamboat leave?" Joey asked as Robbie felt a hand slide in his.

"About forty-five minutes. I called ahead for reservations."

"Super!" Joey sounded about to burst, and Robbie laughed with sheer reflected happiness.

The car eventually stopped. His door opened, and he felt Joey take his hand and guide him outside. The parking lot was filled with people, and Robbie heard snippets of conversation as people passed by. He felt Joey take one arm and Arie take the other. Carefully, they walked toward the boat, the scent of the water growing as they approached. "Welcome aboard!!"

Robbie felt the boat rocking slightly as he stepped off the shifting ramp and onto the deck of the boat.

"This is great!" Joey exclaimed from next to him.

"If you get any more excited, you're going to explode." Robbie smiled in what he hoped was Joey's general direction and was rewarded with a slight hug, and he felt Joey sit next to him.

"Why don't you look around? I'll sit here with Robbie," Arie offered, to Robbie's relief. He knew he was just along for the ride and that Joey would stick next to him if he wasn't encouraged to have fun and see things.

"Okay." A loud whistle signaled their departure. "I won't be long."

Robbie touched Joey's hand. He hoped it was Joey's hand. "Take your time and have fun." Robbie heard the whomp, whomp, whomp, of the paddles hitting the water and the creak of the drive shafts as they turned the wheel.

Arie helped him up, and they walked gingerly along the deck, a steady stream of instruction whispered in his ear. He felt them pass inside and the coolness welcomed them as Arie found them a table.

"Would you like a drink?" He heard what he presumed was a waiter. Arie ordered a beer, but Robbie wasn't thirsty.

Love Means … NO Boundaries

"Can I ask you something?" Arie's voice displayed his concern.

"You can ask anything, Arie." He put his hand over his mouth and snickered. "Well, almost anything."

He heard Arie groan softly. "I can tell you like having him here, and I know you missed him." Robbie found himself nodding his agreement. "Have you given any thought to what you want to do?"

"Do, about what?"

"Robbie, think about it. Joey's going to go home in a few days, and you're going to feel just as bad as you did when we left Michigan, maybe worse." Robbie said nothing and Arie continued. "You were miserable for the entire trip home, and I've got to tell you that even Adelle got tired of that funeral music you played for almost two weeks." Arie's mock anger almost made him smile… almost. "I think Joey calling and asking if he could come for a visit was the only thing that really snapped you out of it." Arie's whisper shouting went straight to his spine.

"What should I do?" His head was swimming, and he suddenly felt like he was going to be sick.

"You need to prepare for it and accept it. Enjoy it while he's here, but you'll need to let him go."

Robbie swallowed and heard a glass being set on the table, and he suddenly wished he'd ordered something. His mouth was suddenly so dry.

"I'm sorry. We shouldn't have had this conversation here, but I didn't know when I'd be able to get you alone again."

"It's okay, Arie. You didn't tell me anything I didn't already know, I guess." But the fun he'd been having had definitely drifted away. What was he going to do? He knew one thing—he never wanted to feel that miserably lost again. There were so many things he wanted to ask Arie, but he heard footsteps, and then the chair next to him moved and Joey's scent filled his nose as a hand snuck into his beneath the table. But this time, instead of making him happy, he was filled with loss, knowing Joey was going to leave.

The boat continued its journey along the river, and Joey cajoled him back onto the deck. This was a day he'd remember for a long time: the scent of the water, the movement of the boat, and Joey's light touch against his arm. Slowly, Robbie felt the funk he'd allowed himself to drift into start to lift, and as the ride ended, he found himself smiling again. He could never remain sad when Joey was around; it just wasn't possible.

"Where to next?" Robbie asked as Joey guided him off the boat and back onto dry land.

"I thought we'd go to Windsor."

Robbie found himself smiling broadly. "Cool!"

"What's Windsor?" Joey asked.

"It's the ruins of a huge mansion. You've got to see it," Robbie answered excitedly. "I can remember it from when I was a kid. It's one of my favorite places." Robbie found himself hurrying back to the car in his excitement and soon they were riding again. He knew immediately when they'd arrived.

"Holy cow!" Joey exclaimed as the car stopped.

"It's pretty amazing isn't it?" Arie beamed from the front seat. "The house was built in the 1800s and was the largest house in the antebellum south. It was destroyed by fire in 1890 and only the columns and a few railings remain."

The car doors opened and Joey helped him get out. Robbie stood outside the car and let Joey lead the way. "I love it here."

"Why?" Joey whispered as they walked. "I mean it's beautiful to see, but…."

Love Means ... NO Boundaries

"Just wait." Robbie smiled. "Lead me inside." The ground under his feet became uneven as they stepped onto the grass.

"Okay, you're in the center. What are we waiting for?"

Robbie slipped on his sunglasses and felt the sun on his skin. It was hot and humid, but as he waited a breeze came up, the wind rustling the trees. "Listen." The wind wound its way through tall pillars, whistling and moaning in the bits of railing that still joined some of the columns together. As the wind built, the pitch changed and moved, the sound moving as the wind died again. "It plays music." He felt Joey grow still next to him. The wind came up again and the columns began to play, this time from multiple places at different pitches—a harmony. "This is a place where the building plays music."

"It's beautiful, Robbie." He felt Joey touch his arm. "Thank you both for bringing me here." People came and went around them, visiting the ruins and marveling at the scope of what was left, but Robbie stood quietly, his friend and his lover on either side of him as he listened to the columns play their music.

CHAPTER 9

THE last few days had been fun, and he'd gotten what he'd come for: time spent with Robbie. During the day, they did things together. Sometimes it was just sitting in one of the house's opulent rooms reading to each other or Joey sitting quietly as Robbie played for him. A few times he'd started to feel very restless, but he reminded himself that he wasn't at the farm.

Yesterday, at one point while Robbie was rehearsing, he sneaked off to the kitchen and helped Adelle as she made her famous fried chicken. When Joey asked if she'd show him how, she'd shut the door and sworn him to secrecy before letting him in on how she made her chicken. When they were done, Robbie had just finished rehearsing, and the two of them had an absolute feast. Yes, he was having a good time.

Joey sat in the kitchen, listening as Robbie's violin music drifted through the house.

"That boy is gonna miss you something awful when you go." Adelle continued working, but Joey could hear the concern in her voice.

Love Means ... NO Boundaries

"I know." He did, very acutely. He was going to miss him just as much. The last time they'd parted was so hard, but this time was going to be worse. He knew how he felt about Robbie. There was no doubt this time. His heart was telling him with absolute clarity. "I just don't know how to prevent it. I'd stay if I could, but...." He just couldn't finish.

He heard a splash as a pan dropped into the dishwater. "You'd never be accepted, not really."

"I got that feeling from Claudine." Robbie's mother had been much more pleasant of late, talking to him and being quite nice. Joey thought it was because she'd figured he was leaving soon anyway, and it didn't hurt her to be hospitable. "It's funny, but Robbie was accepted by everyone at the farm."

"How can that be? He was only there for two weeks." She sounded extremely skeptical.

Joey laughed and explained. "We're talking about a farm owned by two gay men, one of whom was raised by a gay father and his partner."

Adelle joined him, snickering at herself. "Good point, Mr. Joey." She got quiet and Joey got up to find Robbie. "Were you serious? The folks you know don't really care where you come from?" Again there was that skeptical tone.

"The folks I know don't," he said, adopting her phrase. "But I live on a farm. Who's to mind, the horses? Personally, I find Robbie attractive because of where he comes from. It's part of what makes him special."

She scooted him out of the kitchen, and he walked through the hall to the music room where Robbie was practicing. As he approached he heard soft voices and saw Robbie and his mother talking. Robbie nodded his head and didn't look too happy. His jaw was set and his body stiff.

When she was done, she patted his knee and stood up, smiling at Joey as she passed on her way to the living room. It must be cocktail hour.

Joey walked in the room and saw Robbie's expression brighten. Robbie always seemed to know when he was nearby. He really liked that. He knew Robbie's senses were acute, but it still surprised him that Robbie knew him even when he stayed quiet. "Did you and Adelle have a good chat?" Robbie patted the seat next to him.

"We did, actually. I really like her. She's really a special person." Joey didn't know what it was. Maybe she was just a good listener, but he felt he could talk to her.

"Growing up, I spent more time with Adelle than I did with my parents. She practically raised me herself. When the blindness started, she's the one who helped me learn Braille and made me stick with it, even when I threw my books at her."

"Why would you do that?" Joey placed a hand on Robbie's, hoping he'd go on.

"Frustration, I guess. I was twelve years old and went from wearing glasses to near complete blindness in less than a year. I was just mad at the world, and I took it out on her, but she patiently put up with all of it." Robbie stopped and rubbed his big, sightless eyes. "I almost gave up the violin. Mama said it was probably for the best, but Adelle wouldn't hear of it. She kept asking me to play, and eventually I gave in and that was that. She showed me I could still play." Robbie sat back on the sofa. "You didn't come in here to listen to that." Robbie wiped his eyes and lowered his hands.

"Sure I did. I want to know everything about you." They grew quiet, and Joey screwed up his courage to ask. "Did Robert and Claudine treat you differently after the blindness?"

Robbie let loose a troubled laugh. "You tell me. You've met them." He continued snickering and not in a nice way. "The biggest change was in my father. When I could see, we did things together, but afterward I don't think he knew what to do. Mama began staying at home more so she could be with me. We didn't do things together. She just tended to hover. Adelle told me once that she thought Mama was afraid of losing me altogether."

That explained a lot of what he'd seen: Claudine doting on Robbie and Robert working and staying away. Joey looked around the room and then got up and shut the large oak pocket doors, closing them into the room.

"I think we need to talk, but I'm not sure how to start." He stepped back to the sofa and sat next to Robbie. "When you left I realized that I loved you, and I was miserable without you. I have to go back to the farm in a few days, and I'd like you to go with me." There, he'd said it. Robbie may turn him down, but at least this time he'd had the courage to ask him properly.

Joey waited for Robbie's reaction. He wasn't expecting an answer right away, and he grinned when Robbie's face broke into a smile. "You're serious?"

"Of course I'm serious." Joey couldn't stop smiling and felt himself bouncing with excitement and hope.

Then he saw Robbie's smile fade. "I can't." Joey felt like he'd been punched in the gut. Only Robbie's hand on his stopped him from getting up and leaving the room. "Joey, I'd be no use in the farm. I can't help or contribute. I'd just be in the way."

"Bullshit!"

"I would, and you know it. I can't help. Not really. Besides, Eli and Geoff don't need me in their house as well." Robbie's arguments sounded good, but they didn't hold water, not with him.

Joey had the strangest feeling Robbie wasn't telling him everything. "I don't think that's the reason, because you know if I brought you home, Eli and Geoff would be as happy as me. So why don't you tell me the real reason?" Is it because you don't love me enough?" God, he hoped it wasn't that.

"No, of course not!" Heat showed in Robbie's voice. "It's just that this is my home." They were back to that. "Maybe you could stay here."

"You know I can't." Joey softened his voice. "I really want… I *need* you to come back with me."

Joey watched as a number of emotions passed across Robbie's face, and Joey took heart in knowing he didn't say no outright. "Why is my coming with you so important? Is your life more important than mine?"

Joey swallowed hard and thought before answering. "No. If anything, your life is more important, which is why you need to come back with me."

Robbie's face contorted in confusion. "You're not making sense."

"Yes, I am."

"Then tell me why?"

Joey searched for the right words and finally said what he was feeling. "Because I want my Robbie back." The words tumbled out.

"Your Robbie?" His eyes blazed with sightless fire.

"Yes, my Robbie. I want the Robbie who rides horses with me, who begged me for a motorcycle ride. I want the Robbie who spent afternoons helping me plant a garden and drove a tractor." Joey's voice became louder, and his words tumbled out. "I want the Robbie who can find his way through the house without being led everywhere. But mostly, I want the Robbie who told me that I was beautiful and that the only boundaries that really matter are those you place on yourself." Joey kept going, afraid that if he stopped he'd never be able to say what he needed. "I went on the riverboat, and we spent time in town. People turned and looked, and some

170

stared. Do you think I would have done that at all before I met you?" Joey took a heaving breath and continued. "You showed me that I could do anything and that I was holding myself back by hiding myself away." Robbie looked shocked, but Joey'd come too far to stop now. "Then I came down here and saw the man I loved, the daredevil I knew, unable to find his way around his own home."

"They're just trying to help." Robbie's response sounded feeble.

"How? By coddling you and not letting you do things for yourself?" Joey felt himself getting angry on Robbie's behalf and consciously tried to calm himself down as he heard his voice resonate through the large room.

"I love you, Robbie, more than I've loved anyone in my life. And I love you for you. Remember what you did at the farm? Remember that fun being together, the feeling that you could do anything?" Joey's voice became quiet. "Remember what it felt like to be my Robbie without all the boundaries?"

Joey leaned to him and kissed a dazed Robbie gently. "It's your decision. If you decide to stay, I'll respect it." Joey waited for Robbie's reaction, but he gave nothing away. He knew one way to find out. "Would you play for me?"

Robbie shook his head. "I think I'd rather be alone right now."

Joey didn't know what to think, wondering if he'd pushed too hard. Getting up he walked to the door and turned before opening it, looking for some sort of sign from Robbie, but there was nothing, only a set jaw and very confused look. Slowly he opened the door and heard conversation and the tink of ice cubes in glasses.

"Joey, is that you?" Robert asked from the living room. "Are you and Robbie joining us for cocktails?"

As he walked toward the living room, he heard the violin, and he stopped, listening. He hoped to get some insight, but the music betrayed nothing, absolutely nothing at all. Joey didn't think he could really face Claudine, but sucked it up and went into the living room.

He didn't talk much during cocktail hour and at dinner. Instead, he found himself looking at Robbie constantly, kicking himself over and over for pushing too hard. Robbie said almost nothing at dinner either, but thankfully Claudine had some restoration project that she was planning with the columns on the front porch, and she went on about it almost the entire meal. When it was over, Robbie got up, and Adelle appeared at the door. Joey got up, too, but she gave him a look, and he backed away. He could only watch as she led Robbie back into the music room. Minutes later, violin music filled the house.

Joey stood in the doorway and watched Robbie play. A tap on the shoulder made him jump slightly. "Mr. Joey, you need to give him time."

"Did he say anything to you?" He turned, drawing his gaze away from Robbie.

She shook her head no. "He didn't have to." She looked around and then tilted her head toward the kitchen like some sort of spy. Without another word, she bustled down the hall and through the back kitchen door. Joey watched Robbie for a few minutes, but he never stopped playing, his concentration fully on his music. With a sigh, Joey pulled himself away.

Adelle was cleaning up, although how she could make such a fabulous dinner and leave almost no mess behind was a wonder. "Sit down. I'll bring you a cup of coffee."

Joey did as instructed, and to his surprise, Adelle seated herself across the table with her own mug. "This is none of my business, but I love that boy out there like he was my own. I helped raise him since he was in diapers, and it nearly killed me when he went blind." Joey opened his mouth, but she tutted softly. "Let me say my piece."

Love Means ... NO Boundaries

Joey nodded, and she went on. "I know you asked him to go back with you." She must have seen Joey's surprise because she elaborated. "In this house, I never hear anything, but I know everything, if you get my meaning."

Joey nodded. He thought he understood, at least.

"So I'm gonna break my own rule and say something. He's confused and scared. Here he's taken care of and watched out for, maybe too much, but here it's safe, and he's safe, and he knows it. Going with you is taking a big chance." She took a drink and set the mug down again to let her words sink in. "I know you love him, and he loves you. Lord, how that boy loves you, so don't doubt it no matter what he decides. Change is harder for him—things tend to sneak up on him 'cause he can't see 'em coming."

The door to the kitchen opened, and Claudine stuck her head in, frowned slightly, and then closed the door again. Adelle got up and went back to work without saying another word, and Joey handed her his cup, leaving the kitchen, making sure Claudine saw him as he walked though the hall to the music room. Quietly, so he wouldn't break Robbie's concentration, he sat down on one of the chairs and listened, making no sound, not even shifting on the chair.

For hours the music flowed beautifully and seemed a part of his lover. The lines and cadences filling the room, and Joey seemed to grow with them as the notes wound their way into his heart. As the last note faded away, Joey saw Robbie's chest heaving as he lowered his violin, exhausted, and seemed once again to be aware of his surroundings. Putting the instrument in its case, Robbie got up and made his way to the far door, quietly summoning Adelle. It was then Joey realized Robbie didn't know he was there. Before, no matter how quiet he'd been, Robbie always seemed to sense him, but not this time. Maybe whatever magic they'd had that allowed for that was now gone. He didn't know, but he was surprised at how empty he felt, like he'd lost something precious.

Joey watched as Adelle guided Robbie out the door, and a few minutes later he heard Robbie say good night to his parents, followed by their footsteps on the stairs. Joey roused himself from the chair and said his good-nights as well.

In his room, he cleaned up and climbed into bed, the sounds of the Southern night making themselves heard through the windows. Every noise in the house gave him hope, but as the hall lights faded and the house quieted, for the first time since he arrived, he spent the night alone.

ROBBIE heard Joey come upstairs and stop outside his door. He'd been relieved when he didn't knock and went to the room across the hall. He wasn't punishing him. He just needed to think, and he couldn't do that when Joey was next to him, touching him, loving on him. So Robbie got himself undressed and climbed into his bed. He heard a soft knock and his father's voice from the doorway. He was so surprised. He couldn't remember the last time his father had stopped by like this. "I'm sorry, you're in bed." It sounded like his father was going to leave.

"It's all right, Papa." Robbie repositioned himself on the bed. It didn't matter to him, but he knew it made others more comfortable if he was looking in their direction as they spoke. "I wasn't asleep."

Robbie heard his father's heavy footsteps across the floor, and then the bed dipped as he sat down. "It's been a long time since I was in here… too long. Maybe if I'd spent more time with you, you wouldn't be… you know." He heard his father swallow. "Gay."

"Papa."

"Robbie, would you call me Dad? You're a man now, and you need to act like it. Papa is for children, and I think it's time we all stop treating you like one."

Love Means ... NO Boundaries

That was a bit of a shock. "Pa—I mean—Dad, you didn't do anything to make me gay. It's just the way I am. You and I tossing the ball or going fishing, or rastling alligators together." He smiled and hoped his dad was smiling, too. "It wouldn't have changed anything. I'd still be both gay and blind."

"You're not making this easy on me, are you?"

"Why should I? In the last ten years, we've spent almost no time together." Robbie suddenly wasn't feeling particularly charitable. After all his father had largely ignored him for the past decade and it hurt. "Why, Dad? What did I do?"

He felt his father's hand on his shoulder. "Nothing, Son. You didn't do anything. I just didn't know how to deal with your blindness, and as time passed, it got harder and harder. Before I knew it, you were grown, and I didn't know you at all any more."

"So why now, Dad?"

"It took guts to tell your mother and I you were gay, and it took even more to invite the man you're obviously in love with to visit us. I guess I realized that suddenly you weren't a child anymore. You're a man, and you need to act like one and take responsibility like one."

Robbie listened and wondered where his father was going. "Meaning what, Dad?"

"Meaning I know Joey has probably asked you to go back with him."

"And…."

"And," Robbie thought he heard a smile in his father's voice. "I remember when I first met your mother almost thirty years ago. Her father put me through hell, but she was the most beautiful and interesting girl I'd ever met. It took me years to get up the courage to ask her for a date and after that I trailed around after her like a dog for two years until I convinced her to marry me. And the day she married me was the happiest day of my life until about two years later when we had you." He sounded proud and sad at the same time. "The point is that I put up with your grandfather for years because I loved your mother and there was never a day it wasn't worth it."

"I don't understand what you're getting at, Dad."

"I know I'm not saying it very well, but what I mean is that love, true love, is worth what you have to pay for it." Robbie felt the bed rise as his father got up. Then he was hugged, tightly. "I'm proud of you, Robbie, and I love you very much." Footsteps followed, a switch clicked, "and you've got more courage than anyone I know." Then his door closed.

"Wow." Robbie was happily stunned. Was his father telling him to go? Somehow he didn't think that was it. Maybe he was telling him he'd support him if he decided to go. His head started to ache, and he settled back into the bed, his mind racing with all kinds of thoughts and questions.

Would his parents let him go? It sounded like his father wouldn't fight him, but his mother was another matter. When he was gone, she called all the time, and since he'd been back, she had been her usual smothering self. Only Joey's visit had gotten her to back off, at least somewhat. He knew she could be a lioness when it came to him.

Would Eli and Geoff want him? Joey said they did, and his mind floated back to Eli's goodbye. "You're always welcome here." It was said with such heart.

What would he do there? Money wasn't an issue. He had a trust fund that he could live off of the rest of his life. But could he pull his weight on the farm? That was the problem—well, one of the problems—that he just couldn't get past. He knew he couldn't contribute in a meaningful way. He didn't at home either, but at least he was family.

Did he love Joey? Yes, without a doubt. Did he love him enough to take the chance? Did Joey love him enough to saddle himself with a blind partner? Questions, questions, and more questions kept running through his head over and over.

In the wee hours of the morning after plenty of sleepless thought, he came to his decision. Good or bad, he knew what he had to do for his own happiness—and more importantly—Joey's.

He almost got out of bed and went to Joey's room, but couldn't. Not yet.

In the morning, sounds inside and outside the house woke him from a restless sleep. It was still early, but he got up anyway and felt his way to the door and across the hall. He didn't knock, just opened the door and walked in, hearing Joey's soft snores coming from the bed.

Walking toward the sound, he touched Joey's skin, feeling the heat against his palm. The breathy snores didn't stop, but Joey clutched his hand, pulling it to him the way a child clutches a stuffed toy.

Robbie smiled as he was pulled closer and onto the bed. Then he heard Joey's laughter, and he knew he'd been had. Arms and legs wrapped around him, and he quickly found himself in Joey's bed, the two of them giggling softly.

His soft laughter quickly turned to a quiet moan as he felt Joey's legs seeking out his own. Hot skin slid along his, and he felt Joey's fabric-encased excitement against his hip. His mind clouded as desire began to take over.

"Joey," he said through his passion-induced haze. "Please, I need to talk to you."

The hands stilled and the bed shook slightly as Joey's weight shifted. "Is something wrong?" Voice wary.

"No. Yes. I need to talk to you." He didn't want to do this here, but he had to before this went too far.

The bed shifted again and some of Joey's warmth slipped away as his touch lessened. A deep sigh filled the room. "I know what you're going to say—you're not coming back with me." The whisper of heartbreak.

"I can't." Robbie felt his heart tearing as he said those two small words. Arie was right. It hurt worse than the last time, much worse. Tears stung his eyes, and he found himself unable to say more. Joey's weight shifted toward him, and he had to get away. Sliding off the bed, he made his way to the door, closing it behind him as he made his way across the hall, shutting his door and locking it. He managed to make it to the bed before completely falling apart.

He heard Joey's footsteps outside the door, heard Joey knocking and calling to him. He couldn't face him, not like this. What he was doing was the hardest thing he'd ever done in his life, but he had to do it for Joey's sake.

Eventually he heard Joey step away from the door, and he managed to get himself together. A key turned in the lock, and he was about to tell Joey to go when he heard Adelle's voice. The door opened, and he heard her step in the room. "It's okay, baby. It's okay." Then he was being held in her arms and rocked like a child.

Finally Robbie got himself under control, and Adelle released him, saying nothing more, and then bustled around the room, handing him his clothes before squeezing his shoulder and then leaving the room. Somehow Robbie got himself cleaned up and dressed. Now that he felt more in control, he hoped he could explain things to Joey. He was about to leave the room when his door opened, and he heard a rush of footsteps.

Love Means ... NO Boundaries

"What happened?" It was Arie.

"Joey asked me to go back with him, and I told him I couldn't." He swallowed the lump and tried to keep under control.

"What? Why would you do something so stupid?" Arie didn't give him a chance to answer. "I saw Joey downstairs, and he looks worse than you, if that's possible."

"He deserves more."

"More than…." Arie paused. "You didn't? Jesus, Robbie, for a guy who can't see, you sure are blind." Arie began to laugh. "That came out wrong."

"Ya think!"

"What I meant was that… look, I thought I was in love with you and gave Joey a lot of grief because I thought he was taking you away. But I realized I wasn't in love with you as much as I loved you and wanted to protect and take care of you."

He crossed his arms in front of his chest. "Yeah, so!" He wanted to feel better, not get a lecture.

"So Joey loves you like he's in love with you. He doesn't want you to take care of you or protect you, or whatever you think he wants. Joey loves you for you—for who you are. Yes, Joey knows you're blind, but he loves you and sees you for you."

"How do you know this?" Robbie could feel his resolve crumble.

Robbie heard Arie snicker. "I can tell by the way he looks at you." Arie dodged as Robbie tried to slap him and missed. "I'm serious. Whatever reason you concocted in that beautiful mind of yours, you need to make sure it's a good one, because you're about to make both of you miserable." He heard Arie walk toward the door.

"Are you telling me I should go?" Robbie was getting more and more confused by the second.

The footsteps stopped. "I'm saying that you need to truly decide what you want. Not what you think I want or your mother wants, or what's best for Joey. He's told you what he wants because he asked you to go with him." The floor creaked softly beneath Arie's weight as he heard the door open. "We'll be waiting for you downstairs." Robbie heard the door close forcefully.

Robbie sat on the edge of the bed holding his head. He'd spent much of the night trying to figure out what he should do, and now he was more confused than ever. He'd hurt Joey, and he was miserable at the thought of not being with him. He thought he'd done the right thing, but now…. His head throbbed, and his heart hurt, that was all he knew for sure.

CHAPTER 10

HE HEARD the announcement calling his flight and got up from his seat, handing the gate attendant his boarding pass before walking down the jetway. A few minutes later, his bags were stowed, and he was seated. People moved around him, but Joey's thoughts were miles away. Saying goodbye to Robbie on the front porch, beneath those grand columns, was the hardest thing he'd ever had to do.

The flight attendants made their announcements, and he felt the plane begin to move away from the gate and make its way out toward the runway. More announcements and then they sped up and lifted into the air. His stomach was tied in knots, and he did his best to calm himself. He was going home. Back to Geoff and Eli, his family, and back to the farm and animals that he loved so much.

As the plane leveled off, the lack of sleep over the last few days caught up with him, and he closed his eyes, trying to keep himself calm, and somehow, miraculously, he settled into a nervous sleep.

He awoke to the plane shaking and jumping, the pilot making an announcement that everyone was to fasten their seatbelts. Rain pelted the now dark windows as Joey felt the plane descend. He let out a small sigh of relief as the wheels touched the ground after the rough approach. His flight schedule had him routed through Cleveland, and as he exited the aircraft, the airport departure screens were flashing "delayed" on almost every flight.

Hours passed and still most flights were delayed. Heavy storms were keeping almost everything grounded. The delays turned to cancellations, and Joey was stuck. The airline could get him on a flight in the morning, but he had hours to wait. Taking out his phone, he called the farm, told Eli what had happened, and then settled into a quiet section of the airport to wait out the night.

When he woke in the morning, his first thought was of Robbie. He pulled himself together and heaved his body off the carpet. Finding a bathroom, he got himself cleaned up as best he could and checked on his flight. What a difference a day makes. The sun was out and his flight was called on time. In an hour he'd be landing and few hours later, he'd be home.

This flight was completely uneventful, and Joey found himself in the car, his luggage stowed in the trunk, driving north down the freeway, toward the farm, toward home. Two hours later, he turned the corner on US10 at the flashing light, the final leg of the journey. Ten minutes later, he pulled into the familiar drive and parked in his usual spot.

"Joey!" He heard the back door open and saw Eli rush out of the house and he was immediately engulfed in a hug. "You had us worried." He opened the trunk, and Eli helped him carry his luggage inside. "I've got food on, so sit down, and tell me all about the trip."

The suitcase thunked on the floor, and he found himself looking around the familiar farmhouse. It wasn't fancy or grand and it certainly wasn't filled with antiques and expensive things, but it was home, and it was beautiful. "Is Geoff out helping the guys?"

Love Means ... NO Boundaries

Eli turned toward the stove and began heating up some food. "No, he's running errands. He'll be back in a few hours." The smell of whatever Eli was cooking made Joey's mouth water, and he poured a cup of Eli's sensational coffee and took his mug to the table. "So how was Natchez?"

Joey sipped his coffee and told Eli all about his trip as Eli dished up food and set a plate in front of him. Joey tucked in, not realizing just how hungry he was. Eli filled Joey in on everything that had happened on the farm. As he ate Rex ambled into the kitchen, tail wagging as he placed his nose on Joey's lap, the dog's kittens bounding around their legs.

When he was done eating, Joey yawned broadly, and Eli took his plate. "Take your things upstairs and rest for a while." Joey yawned again as he nodded his agreement and lifted his suitcase, thinking it had gotten heavier in the last hour, and headed upstairs to his room.

It felt so familiar, so good to be home, and yet it was still empty, just like it had been since the day Robbie had gotten on that damned bus. Rather than unpack, he dropped his case next to the dresser. Slipping off his shoes, he laid down on top of the bed. The sounds of the house lulled him to sleep and the summer breeze caressed him in its embrace through the open window. He rolled and turned, waking occasionally, but finally resting properly for the first time in days. He was home. No matter what, at least he was home.

He woke hours later—not to noise or because he was fully rested, but because the heat of the day had warmed the room. Yawning widely he made himself get up.

Still yawning and slightly bleary-eyed, Joey wandered through the house, searching for someone, but it was empty and quiet. As he listened he heard the sound of squeals and laughter drift on the breeze. Stifling another yawn, he grabbed a bottle of water from the fridge and walked outside and across the yard to the barn. There was someone, well, plenty of someones, he needed to say hello to.

Noble heads perked up as he approached, and Tiger bounded across his paddock, stopping at the fence for a nuzzle and a pat. He actually looked disappointed as he sniffed Joey's pocket. "Sorry, boy, no treats. I'll have one for you later, I promise." He patted the long black neck and then moved on to greet Twilight and the other horses.

Laughter, louder now, mixing with Eli's patient voice, told him that a lesson was in progress. Smiling to himself he wandered out o the ring and watched as Eli gave a group lesson to some of his beginners. The kids were just as excited as they could be. "Keep your heels down, Jimmy," Eli called, as he walked to where Joey stood leaning against the fence. "Have a good nap?"

He nodded. "Needed it." Joey looked over the group as they trotted around the ring.

"Carrie Anne, let the horse guide you." Eli nodded to Joey and walked to where Carrie Anne and Peanut were trotting, and Joey watched as Eli gently corrected her form.

A sound behind him captured his attention, and he turned around. Looking through the barn, he saw Geoff's truck as two figures walked toward him. "Geoff!" He called and waited for him to step from the darkness of the barn. As they did, Joey's breath caught in his chest. "Robbie!" He found himself rooted on the spot and waited until Geoff brought him close. "I wasn't expecting you for a few weeks." Secretly, he was afraid Robbie would change his mind, and he'd refused to allow himself to believe he was coming. Now Robbie stood in front of him, so close he could feel his breath, and then he was in his arms, kissing him.

"Oooh, kissing." A small voice behind them called and the other kids all made similar noises, like they'd been caught doing something naughty. He backed off with the kissing as both of them began to laugh.

"I caught a flight early this morning and called Geoff. He told me you were delayed, something about the weather."

"If I'd known, I'd have waited for you." Joey looked over at Eli who beamed back at him. Of course the little bugger had known and hadn't told him.

"After you left Mama and I had a long talk. I think Dad talked to her first, though."

"I hope it was better than the shouting match I heard just before I left." When Robbie first told his mother he was going to be leaving with Joey, she made some sounds he hadn't thought were humanly possible.

"She calmed down. She still tried to talk me out of going, but—" Robbie's voice was momentarily drowned out by a chorus of laughter and applause as Eli wrapped up the class. "I told her I was a man now and needed to make my own decisions."

Joey couldn't help smiling, "What did she say?"

"Nothing."

"Then what convinced her?"

"I told her what you said to me about boundaries and that it was time I expanded mine. I think for the first time she might have realized that maybe by sheltering me, she wasn't helping me." Robbie rested his head on Joey's shoulder. "But don't be surprised if we get a call that she's coming to visit soon." Robbie tried to keep himself from laughing, but failed. "I told her that would be okay and asked her if she knew how to ride."

Joey picked up on Robbie's mirth. "I can just see your mother in full makeup, perfect hair, flying across a field on a horse."

Robbie's laughter increased. "That's the best part. His voice got all haughty and she said"—Robbie mimicked her perfectly—"'Of course I can ride. My granddaddy was in the cavalry'." They both broke into peals of laughter.

"How about you?" Joey asked as his laughter abated.

"How about me, what?"

"You feel up to a ride?" Robbie's scent filled his nose, drowning out everything else.

"Oh yeah, I could use a good ride." Robbie kept his face serious, and Joey did a double take before leading them toward the barn. Robbie waited while Joey saddled Twilight. Then he got Robbie mounted, joining him in the saddle before hands held him by the waist. When they were ready, a click of his teeth started Twilight forward.

They rode across the field, and Joey felt Robbie's hands begin to wander, first over his chest and then sliding beneath his shirt, gliding over his skin. "Could you stop a minute?" Wondering what Robbie had in mind, he stopped and felt Robbie fidget behind him. His shirt was lifted and after some fumbling, pulled off him. Then he felt Robbie's skin press to his back with a soft sigh breathed into his ear. "That's better."

Joey had to agree, it was much better, and it got better yet when Robbie began stroking his skin, hands sliding over his chest, fingers circling his nipples. Joey enjoyed the touch, pressing lightly back against Robbie's smooth skin.

Twilight kept walking, and Joey did his best to pay attention as Robbie's hands kept up their magic. He felt Robbie's lips against his shoulder and found himself stretching into the touch. Robbie's hand slid down his chest and stomach, but instead of stopping, they kept going. Nimble fingers popped the buttons on his jeans and a hand slid down inside, gripping him and stroking along his now rigid length. "Robbie."

Love Means ... NO Boundaries

"What?" he asked innocently in Joey's ear. "You want me to stop?" They entered the shade of the woods.

"Oh God." The fabric of his jeans parted farther and another hand joined the first, cupping his balls as he was stroked lightly. "Fuck, Robbie."

"That's what I'm hoping for, Joey." The horse walked on, and Joey turned them at the creek, continuing until they reached the clearing. He hadn't come prepared with anything to ease the way, but as soon as Robbie got off Twilight, he began opening his pants, shoving them to the ground.

Joey spread the blanket he'd brought out of habit onto the ground and pulled Robbie to him. Shoes slipped off, pants crumpled in a pile, and mouths found each other as bodies pressed together. "I'm sorry I put you through all that." Robbie panted between kisses.

"Nothing to be sorry for. You're here, and that's all that matters." Words failed them as they made love in the shade, replaced by pleas and cries of need as Robbie's inner lion came to the fore. His hands seemed to be everywhere at once and lips sucked and licked nose to knees. When Robbie took him between his lips, Joey thought his head was going to explode.

"I want you, Joey." Robbie let Joey's cock slip from his lips as he felt his way up Joey's body.

"I don't have anything." The look of disappointment was too much for Joey. "Okay, on your back. We'll do this the old fashioned way."

Robbie complied, resting on the blanket. "What's the old fashioned way?"

"Roll over and I'll show you."

A questioning look flitted across Robbie's face as he rolled over. Joey settled between his long legs, hands sliding from knees to thighs, and as Robbie spread his legs, Joey zeroed in and slid his tongue along Robbie's cleft. "If this is the old fashioned way," Robbie's voice broke as Joey teased the tiny indentation. Robbie threw his head back and let lose a growly whimper, forgetting his words as he cried out his pleasure.

The musky flavor exploded on his tongue, Robbie's flavor, as he thrust deep, smiling as Robbie writhed and jumped beneath him. Fingers and tongue alternated as whimpers and cries filled the clearing, competing with the brook for attention. Joey knew where to touch and touch he did, eliciting cries of excitement that built on each other as he massaged that special place inside his lover.

Feeling the muscle relax, he positioned himself and slowly entered Robbie's body, joining them together, sinking into Robbie's body.

"Oh God," Robbie moaned, as Joey sank deep inside him. Joey crushed his eyes closed as Robbie's voice, combined with the heat of his lover's body, threatened to pull him over the edge. Stilling himself and breathing, Joey began to move, slowly at first, his hips gliding as Robbie's heat radiated up to him. Stretching on top of Robbie, their lovemaking built slowly and steadily, Robbie crying out and Joey panting and gasping for breath each time he looked at the beautiful, giving, loving man beneath him.

Pressure built inside him, and he could tell by Robbie's cries that he was getting close as well. Joey changed angles slightly, and Robbie keened, filling the woods with the sound of his release as Joey added his own cry of passionate pleasure.

TWO weeks—he'd been back at the farm for two whole weeks, and he was exhausted and exhilarated. He'd been a fool for thinking he couldn't contribute. They'd been keeping him busy almost every minute of the day, and he loved it.

Descending the stairs behind Joey, Robbie unconsciously counted the steps, with Rex right on his heels. He wasn't sure where the kittens were, but they weren't too far behind to be sure. At night, his and Joey's bed seemed like a menagerie. He often disturbed a sleeping body when he stretched his legs, but he never had to worry about being warm enough, that was for sure.

The house had become so familiar; he didn't need to think any more. He just knew where he was. Reaching the bottom of the stairs, he turned and walked through to the kitchen, hearing the morning news on the television as he passed through the living room.

"Robbie." He heard a sip of what he assumed was coffee and a half slurp that could only have been made by Geoff. "Will you be able to run down that loan information from the bank today?"

He pulled out a chair, his chair, and sat down. "Sure. Is the information on your desk?"

"Usual spot."

Robbie's concerns about Geoff and Eli welcoming him into their home had been laid to rest pretty quickly. Geoff had filled the office with every tool Robbie could need. A high-end Braille embosser, a second PC complete with top notch speakers and the best text to speech software available, Braille keyboard, and anything else Geoff could think of. He'd even started referring to Robbie as his able assistant.

"Okay, I'll get on it as soon as the bank opens." He'd found he was quite good at running things down and spent a good portion of his days placing orders and chasing down loose ends for Geoff.

"Thanks. I never really got on with Jenkins, but he really seems to like you."

He usually spent his mornings helping Geoff and his afternoons helping Joey where he could. He'd even figured out where he could help with haying and other big projects. He found he had some limits, but his days were very busy and his nights were wonder-filled.

"Robbie." His attention popped back to the here and now. "Would you like one egg or two?" Eli asked.

"One, please."

He heard Joey sit down next to him, felt Rex settle at his feet, and heard the kittens skitter across the floor. A plate was set in front of him, and Joey explained where everything was and began to eat.

Conversation about the farm and the plans for the day were shared and debated. The back door opened and banged closed as the guys arrived and received their tasks for the day. It was haying season and there was plenty to do.

"Do you have a lot to get in?" Robbie asked as he finished his breakfast.

"Enough to keep us busy all day."

"Then you better get busy, because it's gonna rain."

Forks dropped on plates. "How do you know?" He heard the skepticism in Geoff's voice along with a sudden nervousness.

"I can smell it."

He heard a chair creak. "There's not a cloud in the sky."

"I'm just saying…." He knew what his senses were telling him.

The table got quiet for a while. "Then start making calls to see if you can round up some more help."

Geoff was taking him seriously. How cool was that? Finishing his breakfast, Robbie got up and carefully carried his coffee to the office. After a close call, Eli had gotten him a stainless travel mug for use in the office.

Robbie found the file and listened as his computer began reading off the names and telephone numbers.

As Robbie was finishing the calls, his cell phone rang, playing a tune that used to make him cringe. "Hi Mama." She only called every few days now, a big improvement.

"You're father and I thought we'd come for a visit next month, if that's okay."

"Of course." Robbie was excited for his parents to see the farm. "But you know I'm not coming back with you."

He heard her sigh. "I know. I just miss you something terrible." He heard a voice behind her. "And Adelle says she misses you too."

"I miss all of you as well, but I'm happy and useful here." He went on to tell her all about the things he'd been doing, from riding, to helping Geoff, to convincing Joey to take him on another motorcycle ride, this one uneventful. His rundown was met with silence. "What's wrong, Mama?"

He heard a sniffle, and he almost dropped the phone. "Was I really holding you back?"

Yes! "Only because you're my mama, and you love me. I know you did your best for me and what you thought was best for me."

"But what about your music?"

Robbie beamed into the phone. "That's the best part. I got a job starting in the fall at the middle school in Ludington. I'll be helping to teach kids to play the violin. It's only three days a week, but I can't wait."

The back door opened, and he heard Geoff calling for him. "I have to go, but call me later, and tell me when you wanna come. I love you, Mama."

"I love you, too, and tell that Joey I said hello." He heard a click as she disconnected. *Well, I'll be damned. Maybe by the time she visits, she'll be able to carry on a conversation with him.*

Geoff's footsteps hurried into the office. Did you pack the cooler?"

"It's right outside the back door." And I'm the blind one. "Check it just to be sure." The first time they'd asked him to bring drinks, he'd been so proud of himself. He found the cooler on his own, got the sodas and water from the fridge, and even found the ice in the freezer. What he found out was that all soda cans feel alike and he thought he had a variety, but instead he'd filled the cooler with Diet Coke and only Diet Coke. The guys drank it, but he heard Pete ragging Geoff about letting the blind guy pack the cooler. Since then Eli kept every flavor in a specific place, and there'd been no more complaints.

"How many more people are coming?"

"Four. They should be here soon."

He heard Geoff's footsteps rushing toward the back door. "Thank you!"

"You're welcome," he called back as the back door banged closed.

On days like this, he wished he could do more, but he knew it was best to stay out of the way. Feeling around the desk, he found Geoff's list and began running his fingers over the bumps. He picked up the phone and dialed the bank.

People came and went throughout the morning, hurrying in and out again. Trucks came and went, people yelling and questioning, the yard a bustle of activity. Lunch was sandwiches Eli had made earlier, hastily eaten.

When he'd finished everything Geoff needed, he went upstairs to their room and got his violin and began to play. Content and happy beyond anything he could remember, he let the music from his heart flow through his hands and out to the instrument.

"What song is that?"

Joey's voice startled him, and he stopped playing. "It isn't. I just made it up."

"It sounded happy."

"That's because I am." He set the instrument on his lap. "Don't they need you outside?"

"We just finished." He felt Joey's hands on his legs, and then he was being kissed.

"What was that for?"

"Listen."

Robbie listened and heard the low rumble of thunder in the distance. "I'm glad you finished in time."

"Thanks to you, we had enough help and got it all in." He felt Joey's weight slip away. "I need to help put things away before it rains." Robbie felt another soft kiss and then heard footsteps as Joey left the room and bounded down the stairs.

Picking up his instrument again, he resumed playing and continued until he heard the back door banging closed and the sound of rain on the windows. Sensing he had an audience, he stopped and turned toward the door. "Joey." He knew he was there.

"You're so beautiful when you play. Almost as beautiful as when...."

Robbie felt the violin being lifted from his hand, and he was pressed back against the bed. Rex had been keeping him company, and Robbie felt him jump down to get out of the way. "I love you, Robbie Jameson."

He felt Joey's hand slide under his shirt, the warm palm gliding over his skin, and he began to squirm. His pants were tight, and he wanted to feel Joey's touch. Arching his hips he tried to get Joey's attention a little lower, but it wasn't happening. Those fingers were employed worrying his nipples to points as he was being kissed within an inch of his life.

"Robbie!" A forceful call rang up the stairs.

Joey lifted himself up. "Great timing, Geoff."

"You have a phone call."

Robbie fumbled to his feet and felt along Joey's face, the skin, stubble, and now soft scars glided beneath his fingers. "And I love you." He received a kiss and then made his way to the door, hearing Joey laugh behind him.

"You look like a drunken sailor."

"And whose fault is that?" Getting hold of himself, he made his way downstairs and Geoff handed him the phone.

"Mr. Jameson, I'm Juanita Figueroa with the Mason Lake Intermediate School District." Robbie crinkled his forehead in confusion. "I spoke with Mr. Laughton about creating a therapy riding program at his farm and he agreed. He said I needed to work out the details with you."

"Therapy riding," he whispered to himself.

"Yes." She'd heard him. "These programs give disabled kids a chance to ride a horse. It helps strengthen their muscles and quite frankly, allows many of these kids to do something they never thought they could do."

Love Means ... NO Boundaries

Robbie found himself smiling and jumped slightly when he felt a pair of arms wind around his waist. "What would this entail?" He found himself getting excited about this idea.

"I was hoping we could meet with you and go over everything."

"Sure." This idea really sounded great. "Would you like to come here?"

"We certainly could. Is five tomorrow okay?"

Robbie turned to Joey and filled him in quickly. Joey nodded and smiled his approval completely momentarily forgetting that Robbie couldn't see it. Then caught himself and whispered his answer. "That's fine. We'll be looking for you."

"There's just one more thing. I need to ask if you have experience working with people with physical challenges?"

Robbie began to chuckle. He was needed, loved, and he fit. For the first time, he'd found a place he truly fit. Joey pulled him closer as he concluded the telephone conversation, their bodies melding together as he told him the details. Standing in Joey's arms, the last of those self-imposed boundaries fell away. He knew that with Joey behind him, he could do anything.

Epilogue

JOEY could hardly believe his eyes. "You're doing really well, Cici."

"Thank you, Mr. Joey." She may have braces on her legs, but she was learning to control that horse like a pro. She beamed at him as the small group of five horses and six riders continued slowly down the level trail.

"They're doing really well," Joey whispered to Robbie, who was in his usual place behind him as they led the way on Twilight, with Cici on Belle behind them, followed by three other horses and riders who were each led by a helper.

"I can't believe how well this has worked out," he heard Robbie saying into his ear. Joey knew his lover was listening for any sign of trouble just as he was watching for it.

"Of course it did. You organized it." He had every confidence that anything Robbie set his mind to he could make happen, and Robbie seemed to be starting to believe it himself. They did three therapy riding sessions a week, each with four children. Today it was Cici and three blind children. Cici had been the program's biggest success so far. When she'd first come, she was scared and almost refused to get on the horse, but one look at Robbie sitting behind Joey, and she'd agreed to give it a try. For her first few sessions, they'd had spotters on each side of her, but after her balance improved, her mother had led the horse around the ring.

Joey remembered the day she'd told her mother she could do it herself and that was that. She was riding. Cici still needed help mounting, but that was all.

"Juanita called. They want to add your program to the district's website." He stopped Twilight and craned his neck. Everything was fine, horses happy—they seemed to sense that their riders were special—smiling and laughing. "She said we should give it a name."

"She mentioned it to me too. I was thinking about calling it the No Boundaries Riding Program. "What do you think?"

"It's perfect." Joey turned Twilight around and began heading back to the barn, leading the group on its slow but steady progress. As he passed he watched the helpers leading the horses turn as well. Many were parents, which was wonderful, but the best part was the looks on these kids' faces.

In the barnyard Joey and Robbie dismounted, and Joey helped the kids down, getting a hug from each one as he did. When he lifted Cici down, she hugged him tight, and he felt her brace encased legs around his waist. "If you keep that up, you'll be strong enough and won't need them anymore." He returned her enthusiastic hug and smiled as her mother approached, obviously having overheard his remark.

"That's what the doctor said too." There was a tear in her eye as she beamed at her daughter. "And it's all because of you." She smiled again, and Joey watched as they got in their car, talking about getting ice cream."

"Doesn't get any better than that, does it?"

Joey felt Robbie's hand on his arm. "You heard?" Joey shouldn't have been surprised.

"I hear everything." For a second his accent got heavier, and he sounded like his mother, making Joey laugh.

It didn't take long, and all the horses were back in their stalls, each having had their treat and happily munching hay. Joey saw Eli and Geoff grooming and saddling their horses, a particular look on their faces. They left them alone, walking across the yard.

"It feels cold." Robbie snuggled next to him.

"It's fall, and it's going to get colder," Joey warned as Robbie shivered next to him. "But I think it's the most beautiful time of the year. I wish you could see it." He put his arm around Robbie to warm him.

"Tell me about it."

"All the hills are covered with shades of red and yellow. The oak leaves are brown and some of the maples are orange. The pines are still green. It looks like nature got out her paint brush and colored everything."

He felt Robbie burrow closer and looked at his face, seeing his closed eyes. "I can see it, just like you described."

Joey ran his thumb over Robbie's lower lip. "Let's go inside."

"Okay, as long as you remember your promise."

Joey chuckled softly. He had every intention of keeping it. "I'll keep you warm this winter."

"I was thinking of invoking that promise sooner than that." Joey put an arm around Robbie's waist as he guided him toward the back door. He heard Eli and Geoff behind him, mounting and then the pounding of hooves across the field, gradually getting softer. He could tell Robbie was listening as well and saw by his smile he knew what was happening. "Did they take blankets?"

Love Means ... NO Boundaries

"Yeah." Joey kissed his lover and then opened the back door, and they stepped inside the warm kitchen. "Is that what I think it is?" Joey inhaled deeply, his stomach already growling even though dinner was hours away.

"Yes, I'm makin' your favorite fried chicken." Adelle continued working at the island, making sure the chicken was properly seasoned. "I also whipped up a batch of cornbread." Robbie made a happy, contented sound next to him.

"Are you settling in okay?"

She beamed at him, her eyes shining, "My, yes. The room is just lovely." She kept smiling as she went back to work. About a month after Robbie left Natchez, he'd gotten a call asking if, "You boys could use someone to do the cooking and cleaning?" Joey and Robbie had discussed it with Geoff and Eli, and they'd all agreed that they'd love to have her come.

The four of them had remade one of the bedrooms for her and even done a little moving around so she could have one of the rooms with its own bath. She'd moved in two weeks ago, and just fit right in. She quietly took over the management of the house. Individually they were Mr. Geoff or Mr. Eli, which tickled all of them no end, but on the whole, she referred to them as her boys, which tickled them all even more.

Claudine had been fit to be tied when she found out Adelle was leaving, but she'd gotten over it. She was already on her second replacement.

"Are you boys playing poker tonight?"

"Of course. It's Friday."

"I'll make up some sandwiches then."

"Thank you, Adelle. Are you joining us?" She did her best to look shocked." Len and Chris will be over, and I think Pete, Frank, and Lumpy will be coming too." Joey laughed as Adelle looked like she was going to brain him with the towel, but she broke into a grin.

"I'd prob'ly clean you all out." Somehow, he didn't doubt it. "Now go relax, and let me finish here." They left the room, and Joey settled on the sofa with Robbie reclining next to him, legs across his lap. Joey pulled off his lover's socks and began rubbing his feet to a chorus of soft, contented sighs.

"How were your students today?" Robbie worked three mornings a week at the middle school teaching violin.

"Much better. They're making progress, and they've learned they can't put one over on the blind guy." Initially Robbie had had some issues with a few students, but they'd learned pretty quickly that he didn't need to see them to know what they were doing. "They're good students and a few of them are very talented. Our first concert is in December. Do you think you'll come?"

Joey ran his hand up Robbie's calf, tickling him behind the knees. "Of course I'll come." He leaned forward, kissing him softly.

"Hey, careful of the claws." Robbie scolded one of the kittens as it jumped down onto his chest. Completely ignoring him, she curled up and proceeded to burrow against Robbie's shoulder, purring like a jet engine as he began to stroke her.

"Do you ever miss home?" Joey worried that Robbie had given up a lot to come here with him.

"If you mean Natchez, sometimes. It was nice when Mama and Dad visited, though I was glad they left too." Robbie paused. "If you're asking if I have any regrets, then the answer is no. And just so you understand, this is my home. You are my home."

Don't miss the other **Love Means...** Novels
by ANDREW GREY

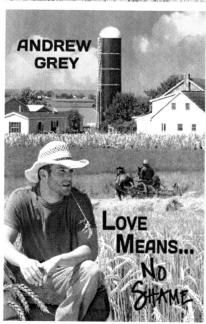

http://www.dreamspinnerpress.com

ANDREW GREY grew up in western Michigan with a father who loved to tell stories and a mother who loved to read them. Since then he has lived throughout the country and traveled throughout the world. He has a master's degree from the University of Wisconsin-Milwaukee and works in information systems for a large corporation. Andrew's hobbies include collecting antiques, gardening, and leaving his dirty dishes anywhere but in the sink (particularly when writing). He considers himself blessed with an accepting family, fantastic friends, and the world's most supportive and loving partner. Andrew currently lives in beautiful historic Carlisle, Pennsylvania.

Visit Andrew's web site at http://www.andrewgreybooks.com and blog at http://andrewgreybooks.livejournal.com/. E-mail him at andrewgrey@comcast.net.

Contemporary Romance by ANDREW GREY

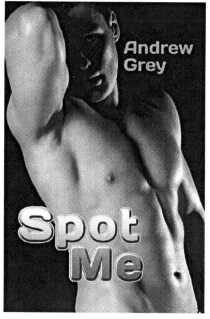

http://www.dreamspinnerpress.com

Contemporary Romance from

DREAMSPINNER PRESS

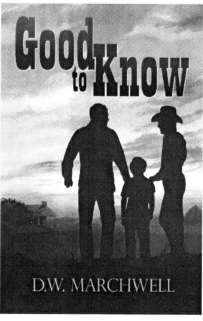

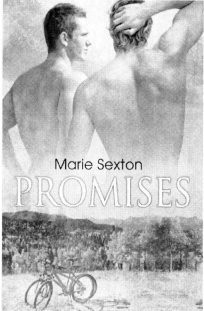

http://www.dreamspinnerpress.com

Contemporary Fantasy by ANDREW GREY

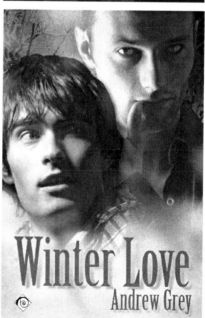

http://www.dreamspinnerpress.com

Breinigsville, PA USA
05 March 2010
233678BV00003B/12/P